MW01113301

Annie Oakley Mystery

By William Baer

Published by Winged Publications

Editor: Cynthia Hickey
Cover image: Courtesy of The National Annie Oakley Center

ISBN-13: 978-1-962168-75-5

For my family and friends

"I shoot a little."
– Annie Oakley

1. The River

Monday, March 12, 1900

I was waiting, at the moment, for the most famous woman in the world.

(With sincere apologies to her majesty, Queen Victoria.)

I was sitting astride Adler, patiently and rather comfortably, on the banks of the Yantokah River, when I saw someone falling from Centre Bridge.

My heart compressed within my chest, as a body, a person, clearly a woman, dropped through the sunlight and smashed to the rocks below. I felt terrified in a way that I'd never previously experienced, and for those initial moments, I sat frozen in my saddle. I've always believed that fear, no matter how reasonable, should never be submitted to or fully tolerated. But it's also true that I'm just a fifteen-year-old girl, although, as the vanity glass reminds me each morning, I'm rapidly transforming into a young woman, and I feel that I should definitely behave as such.

I immediately guided Adler to the stone walls of the bridge, dismounted, and bent over the motionless body. Miss Dalton, the town's much-admired elderly librarian, lay stretched out on her back with her legs crushed and eerily contorted. There was no light in her eyes. Nothing whatsoever. No trace of the beneficent spirit that had always shone from within. I knelt down, avoided her lifeless eyes, and found the carotid artery in her neck, just as my father, my adoptive father, Dr. Matthew Carlyle, had shown me. She was still warm but pulseless. She was dead, and there was nothing more that I could do.

It was just the two of us, all alone on the bank of the river, and I felt that I might cry. Then I heard thundering hooves approaching from behind me. I didn't turn around because I knew who it was. No one else in Franklin could ride a horse like that.

When she was upon us, I turned myself a bit, looking up at Miss Annie Oakley.

Earlier this morning, I'd gone to the old cemetery to visit the grave of the mother I'd never known. Afterwards, I rode over to the river, as I did most mornings, to meet with Mrs. Butler (Annie Oakley) for an hour's trot-and-gallop around Nutley and the surrounding area. Today, since I'd arrived a bit early, I was still thinking about the mother I'd never known when what happened at the bridge had happened.

"Is she dead?"

Annie has a soft and lovely voice, even under duress.

"Yes."

"Are you all right, Lizzie?"

"Yes."

We heard the dog.

Rusty, Miss Dalton's ever-companion, some kind of terrier mix, was making his way towards the dead body of his mistress. He seemed to be limping.

"Did the dog fall?" Annie wondered.

I didn't know.

When I shrugged, we both looked up at the high stone bridge. Maybe the dog had found its way down the embankment.

"That's a peculiar wound," Annie pointed out.

I looked closer and saw the dog's gashing head wound.

"Maybe he hit his head on the bridge," I suggested.

"Maybe."

She seemed suspicious.

Annie Oakley Butler was the kindest most generous woman I'd ever known, but she was also the thoughtful type, the pensive type, the observant type. Always thinking to herself, always carefully contemplating the world and everything within it, as if attempting to make sense of the world around us.

"Would you alert the sheriff, my dear?"

"Of course."

I remounted Adler, looked down again at poor

Miss Dalton one last time, and rode away. When I was down the bank a bit, I turned to look back. Annie, off her Arabian, was now holding and comforting the injured and bewildered terrier within her arms, probably examining its head wound.

Dear Miss Jane Dalton was my first dead body.

My first mystery.

2. Tutor

Monday, March 12, 1900

Punctually, at 1:00, Mr. Phillip Palmer arrived for his interview.

Previously, Dr. Carlyle, who'd adopted me from the orphanage three years ago when I was twelve, was doing what he did every afternoon right after lunch, reading the newspapers. Reading about the difficulties in the Philippines, the recent Boxer Rebellion, the Yellow Fever death counts, and the lively dispatches from South Africa by someone named Winston Churchill regarding the stalemated Boer War.

As encouraged by my father, as well as Sr. Agnes, I also keep up with such things, but I was far more interested, I'm not ashamed to admit, in the formation of the new baseball league, the American Association, and its potential effects on the upcoming season, particularly the prospects of my beloved New York Giants, who were, I'm ashamed to admit, the second-to-worst team in the National League last year.

Yes, I knew all about the Manilla insurgency, the Boxer Rebellion, the deranged anarchists here at home, and the dreaded Yellow Jack, but like most people I knew (and read about), I was full of optimism and confidence about our brand-new century. America was full of promise! The ramifications of the Panic of 1893 were behind us, businesses were booming, jobs were everywhere, and the seaports were bursting. It was easy to envision a rapidly approaching future where most Americans would have in-house electric lighting, in-house plumbing, in-house telephones, and, eventually, one of those curious automobiles, like the ones that Mr. Ford was building in Michigan.

My father was equally optimistic. For years he'd been a pioneer in antiseptic surgery at St. Michael's in Newark, with a specialization in anesthetics, and he envisioned a much better and healthier future for all Americans.

So did Annie Oakley, who'd been all over the world and all over the country and was now sitting on our living room couch.

At present, her beloved husband Frank was down in Philadelphia on business, and she'd agreed to come next door to observe the Palmer interview. She came, as she often did, with several meticulously beautiful embroideries, being, as she was, a masterful seamstress. As a young girl working with orphans and the insane at the Darke County Infirmary in far western Ohio, she'd been taught fine sewing by the infirmary director's wife. As a result, she designed and needled all of her clothes, including her famous riding and shooting outfits. When she was abroad in England a few years ago, as Mr. Frank once told me, all the London designers were unashamedly copying her designs for their riding habits.

Mr. Palmer entered the room.

He was exquisitely handsome and much younger than I'd expected, maybe twenty-five or so. He shook hands with my father, then nodded politely to both Annie and me on the couch.

He was tall, lean, and trim, with very dark hair and very dark eyes. He wore fine clothing, much finer than one would expect for an in-house tutor, and he wore a gold chain with an expensive-looking watch. It would certainly be difficult for most young girls to take their eyes off Mr. Palmer, and I was no exception.

Miss Hinson, my previous tutor, had fallen in love (which is a perfectly marvelous but unrelated story), and she'd recently moved to Manhattan with her new husband.

The interview commenced.

In truth, despite Mr. Palmer's startling good looks, it was hard to displace my mind from the subject of Miss Dalton's death a few hours earlier, but I did my best to follow Annie's lead and pay attention.

The good doctor thoroughly reviewed the young man's resume and references, asking occasional questions as he did so. Mr. Palmer was a recent graduate of Rutgers with a Latin/Roman specialty, and he'd taught at El Granada Schoolhouse, a few miles south of San Francisco, where he had relatives on his mother's side.

"Which grades?"

"I've taught fourth through eighth."

"With *McGuffey's Readers*?"

"Of course."

The doctor was pleased.

"I should alert you that our Lizzie, although technically at the tenth-grade level, is, in reality, far in advance of that. I would calculate that she's well beyond the twelfth grade."

Meaning college level.

Mr. Palmer looked over at me, nodding politely, and I was glad that I wasn't one of those girls who blushed up a storm.

"I'm fully prepared for that," he said with confidence.

Annie spoke for the first and only time.

"When you were teaching *McGuffey's* level six, what was your opinion of the Defoe selection?"

I was amazed. I knew my *McGuffey's* backwards and forwards, and I was positive that the sixth reader contained no such selection.

"I have the greatest admiration for Mr. Defoe, especially his description of Robinson Crusoe's house."

But that was in the *fourth* reader!

She was obviously testing him, but she said

nothing more, and neither did I.

The doctor continued his interrogations, asking a few pointed biological and scientific questions, even asking, aware of my love of the English novelists, a literary question.

"What's your opinion of the work of Mr. Thackeray?"

"Most accomplished," Mr. Palmer decided, without specification.

"What's your personal favorite novel?"

He mulled a bit.

"I would say Cantell Bigly's *Aurifodina.*"

Whatever that might be!

Really?

Hmm.

Except for that, Mr. Palmer proved to be a highly intelligent young man, and he certainly made a favorable impression, but I did notice, from his glaring McGuffey's error forward, that, unless pressed, he spoke in generalities rather than useful specifics.

When all was said and done, the doctor seemed oddly pleased, and whatever my misgivings, I liked him too. My father and Mr. Palmer stood up and shook hands. Annie also stood up, all five feet of her, and similarly shook the young man's hand.

"It was a pleasure to meet you," he said.

Very natural.

Suave, but not slippery.

Sometimes people don't know how to react around

Annie. Some people overreact, some gush, some ingratiate, some are positively struck dumb, but a good number are remarkably normal, and Mr. Palmer had done his best to fit into the last category.

He was just about to leave when Lawrence Langley, the sheriff's deputy, came rushing into the living room. He was doing his best to remain calm.

"We've arrested a vagrant lurking around Miss Dalton's house, but he won't say a word."

He looked at Annie.

"He says, 'I'll only talk to Annie Oakley.'"

3. Jail

Monday, March 12, 1900

"We brought him in for loitering."

But it was clear that the sheriff's suspicions ran deeper than that.

We were standing in the front room of Sheriff Granger's little office on Chestnut Street. A middle-aged widower, the sheriff was a large and powerful man, which, I'm sure, was quite useful for law enforcement. Not that we have very much crime to "law enforce" in either Nutley or neighboring Belleville.

Earlier today, after looking things over at the river, the sheriff had decided that the death of Miss Dalton was an unfortunate accident. She was well-known to take her late morning walks across Centre Bridge.

"Maybe she slipped," he suggested. "Or maybe there was something with the dog."

Annie waited a moment.

"It looks to me," she pointed out, "like Rusty got

kicked in the head."

The sheriff didn't reject it out of hand, but he was still inclined to believe that it was simply an accident. After all, there hadn't been a murder in Nutley in the past twelve years.

Since the murder of my mother.

But now they'd found this young boy hanging around Miss Dalton's little house, which also served as the town's temporary library and temporary records office.

"You're wondering," Annie asked, "if the boy had something to do with Jane's death?"

"I don't know, Annie. Maybe. The kid was hanging around the house, which is pretty suspicious, and he won't say a word, which is even more suspicious. He just sits in his cell humming a song. Maybe he'll open up for you."

Sheriff Granger opened the door to the back room, and we entered, standing outside the bars. I much appreciated the fact that the sheriff never said, "Shouldn't Lizzie wait outside?" or something like that. Ever since I'd turned fifteen in January, Annie had insisted on treating me like an adult, and it had obviously rubbed off on everyone else in town.

The boy stopped humming.

I reminded myself that I was in the midst of a mystery, and that it was important to remember what Doyle's peculiar detective once said to Watson in "Scandal in Bohemia":

You see but you do not observe.

So, I determined myself to do more than just "see."

The boy sat pitifully in his cell on a small wooden bench. He was dressed in worn yet-not-ragged farm clothes, with a blue-green, long-sleeve flannel shirt. His jet-black hair was disheveled, and he looked both lean and farmer-fit. Even though he seldom looked directly at any of us, it was clear that he was a good-looking young boy, just a few years older than myself, and I felt, I must admit, an immediate and natural attraction. Yes, I'm fully aware that a bit earlier I admitted an attraction for Mr. Palmer, and I certainly don't want to appear the town flirt, a silly adolescent with her heart on her sleeve, but I was now fifteen years of age, and attractive young men were hard not to take notice of.

Annie nodded at the cell's barred door, and the sheriff opened it, and the three of us entered the tiny cell.

"You asked for Miss Annie Oakley, and she's been kind enough to come and visit."

When the boy didn't respond, Annie introduced me.

"This is my friend, Miss Elizabeth."

He shrugged, but he didn't look up. Instead, he stared directly at my hands. Which I didn't mind at all. Sr. Agnes had once told me that I had very pretty hands.

"What's your name?" Annie asked.

He hesitated.

"Well," Annie assured him, "I'm not one to waste my time, young man."

He got the message.

"William Smith."

"From where?"

He hesitated again.

"Upstate. New York."

"Where?"

"Utica."

"Why are you here in Nutley?"

"I'm traveling through. I have family in Union City."

I wasn't convinced, and I doubt that Annie was either.

The boy looked up momentarily.

"Do you know where the 300 Steps are?"

"No, I don't," Annie admitted.

Immediately, the boy seemed to lose interest.

"Do you realize," Annie asked him, "that a woman was found dead today?"

"Yes, ma'am, the sheriff told me so, but I know nothing about it. Nothing. I had *nothing* to do with it."

The sheriff butted in.

"Then why were you at the dead woman's house?"

"I wasn't. I was just passing by."

"That's not true. You were loitering in the area."

The boy shrugged again, and it seemed as though

he was ready to shut himself down completely.

Annie stepped closer.

"William?"

He glanced up then down again.

"Who's George Davis?"

Which seemed a very odd question.

"I don't know."

"Who's the governor of the state of New York?"

He shrugged, as if he didn't know.

"Do you know who I am?"

"You're Annie Oakley."

"Do you know why people know who I am?"

"Because you're famous."

"Why?"

Another shrug.

It seemed to me he had no idea who Annie was.

She gestured at me.

"Do you know who this is?"

He shook his head 'no.'

"Please leave me alone. I've got nothing more to say."

It was perfectly clear that he was done, so we all left in silence, thinking things over.

Two mysteries in a single day!

As we exited the room, I made an interior note to myself: later tonight, write everything down, everything you can remember.

Everything!

4. Kinetoscope

Monday, March 12, 1900

I was sitting in the darkness between a beautiful Lakota Indian and the world's most famous scientist.

We were watching the "flickers" of Mr. Thomas Edison, who was sitting beside his projecting Kinetoscope, a new invention he was calling the Projectoscope, which was projecting moving images of "Miss Little Sureshot of the Wild West" across the living room onto a large white screen set in front of the stone fireplace.

Six years ago, when I was still at the orphanage, Annie and Mr. Frank had gone to Mr. Edison's laboratories in West Orange where they were filmed at the Black Maria. Like all the other Edison "shorts," the film was shown in the immensely popular Kinetoscope peephole parlors in New York City, Chicago, Atlantic City, and elsewhere, where people would pay a nickel to see legendary Annie Oakley blasting away targets, including glass balls tossed by Mr. Frank, which were instantly shot and exploded in the air.

How fortunate I am!

Being nothing more than a little nobody from nowhere who was now sitting in a room with Annie Oakley and Thomas Edison, both good friends of Buffalo Bill, who'd all attended last year's Exposition Universelle in Paris, which, for some curious reason, was celebrating the hundredth anniversary of the bloody storming of the Bastille and introducing the odd-yet-exquisite Eiffel Tower as the entryway to the exposition. Annie, featured with Buffalo Bill's Wild West Show, performed for packed audiences, and Mr. Edison demonstrated several of his latest inventions, including the phonograph.

So, I sat in the darkness near the beam of light, amid our various Nutley friends and neighbors, watching a long line of Edison film strips featuring numerous other well-known celebrities like Sandow the strongman, former boxing champion James Corbett, "Serpentine Dancer" Annabelle Moore, Buffalo Bill Cody, and Turkish dancer Ella Lola.

"I do wonder if that one's appropriate for young Lizzie?" Fanny Langley asked, concerned in her usual good-mannered way.

"It's not nearly as salacious as you might think," Mr. Tom assured her, obviously directing his opinion at my father, Dr. Carlyle, who was also a close friend of the New Jersey inventor.

"I think it'll be all right, Fanny," my father

responded in the darkness. “As long as it’s all right with Lizzie.”

I would have preferred to yell out, “Of course, Dad!” but I opted for a more measured response.

“I trust Mr. Tom’s opinion.”

So that was that.

Then we watched Miss Lola cavorting, spinning, and wiggling around a bit to some unheard music, and I certainly would have to agree with Mr. Edison. Although it was obviously showy, and maybe even a bit vulgar, it was hardly “salacious.”

It did, however, make me wonder what Miss Lola did when she was up on stage and not in front of Mr. Tom’s observing camera.

When the films were over, the lights came on in the living room, and there was much lively discussion about everything we’d seen:

Would Jim Corbett, having lost his title since making the film, have any chance in his upcoming Coney Island bout with heavyweight champion Jim Jeffries?

No one seemed optimistic.

Was Mr. Sandow’s excessively rigorous training regimen and his subsequent and commendable physique actually “healthy”?

“Very much so, I believe,” my father decided. “He looks perfectly trim, and fit, and not at all muscle bound.”

Should Ella Lola be allowed to wiggle around on

American stages?

Most of the women, including me, despite our natural fears of being considered puritanical prudes, said no. The men remained mostly silent, except for my father who clearly agreed with the women.

Earlier, after Mr. Edison had set up his equipment in the living room, the evening began with a lovely tribute to Miss Jane Dalton by my father, Dr. Carlyle. It was, of course, exceedingly sad, and it was followed by several other reminiscences and memorials. Fanny Langley, the wife of the mayor, reminded us, in her usual upbeat way, that Miss Dalton always enjoyed good company, as well as a good time, and that she'd been looking forward to Mr. Edison's visit tonight.

"I have no doubt that Jane would have wanted us to enjoy the evening, which Dr. Carlyle and Mr. Edison have so kindly arranged."

Everyone agreed, and we did exactly as she suggested.

Yet never fully forgetting our sudden and inexplicable loss, as we all enjoyed the demonstration of Mr. Tom's flickers and the animated conversations they stimulated.

Aside from our special guest, Mr. Edison, there were ten of us in the room. Since I'd promised myself to explicate the present story as best I can, I would have to admit that, at the present moment, *all* the people in the room were the most likely suspects (excepting mysterious William Smith who was still sitting in his little jail cell) in the possible murder of Miss Jane Dalton. I fully realize that it might seem far too early for some kind of "suspect list," but it will allow me to also introduce, very briefly, a number of our friends and neighbors, who will, of necessity, have to forgive me for placing their names on the list:

> *Fanny Langley*: the lively, popular wife of Mayor Langley, who, despite being at least a generation younger than Jane Dalton, was a very close friend, along with each of the other ladies who regularly attended Annie's "books and tea" get-togethers every other Sunday afternoon.
>
> *Mayor Warren Langley*: our likeable, much-admired mayor, a dedicated civil servant as well as the director of the Franklin Trust. He's currently leading the effort to officially change the name of the town from Franklin to Nutley, which has unanimous support in the town.
>
> *Veronica Fairfax*: the wife of the much-respected county judge, Owen Fairfax (not in attendance this evening). Always reserved, always elegant, always dignified, Mrs. Fairfax is the only living descendent of a wealthy local family, and she remains the controlling owner of the town's primary supply store. She and her

husband have two grown sons, Keith and Bryan, both of whom work as attorneys in New York City.

Sr. Agnes Marie: the beloved co-director of St. Mary's Orphanage. At the age of three, when I first arrived at the orphanage on the day that my mother was murdered, Sr. Agnes took a special interest in my sorry situation. Throughout my life, she's been both a mentor and a confidante, as well as a motivator, and six years ago, she encouraged Miss Annie's interest in wanting to help me and improve my lot in life.

Deputy Sheriff Lawrence Langley: the good-looking and likeable son of the Mayor and Fanny Langley. Since I've determined to write with as much candor as possible, I think it's appropriate to mention that he's quite fond of me and that the word "infatuated" might not be too strong a word. He's now twenty-two years old, seven years my senior, and I feel obligated to mention that he's rather attractive, and that I've always found his attraction toward me quite attractive.

Theresa Morning Dove: a Lakota archer from the Pine Ridge Reservation in South

Dakota who performs with Annie in Mr. Cody's Wild West Show. She's lovely, reserved, and virtually taciturn. At the age of nineteen, she's quite simply the most beautiful woman I've ever seen in my life. With thick dark hair, high cheekbones, marvelous smile, impeccable skin (despite all her outdoor activity), and everything else. She's also the granddaughter of Annie's late friend Sitting Bull, the victor at Little Big Horn. During the last two years, she's spent part of the winter here in Nutley. As you might expect, Annie and Frank have all kinds of fascinating visitors to their home – marksmen, rough riders, plains Indians, circus and Wild West performers, promoters, reporters, politicians, etc. – but Annie's always taken a special interest in Theresa.

Phillip Palmer: my very well-dressed, exceedingly handsome new tutor, who certainly doesn't know his *McGuffey's Readers* as well as he wants us to believe. To be perfectly honest, I was rather surprised that my father decided to hire him after his interview this afternoon, but he seems very nice, and I like him, so we'll see how it goes.

Sheriff Richard Granger: our hardworking sheriff, who probably shouldn't be on anyone's

> suspect list, but since he's here tonight, I'm including him on the list. The sheriff is a widower with one son, Jimmy Granger, whom I know *very* well.

Also in the room, of course, were Annie and my father, both of whom I've excluded from the list.

Along with Mr. Edison!

Eventually, as the evening wound down, people began to leave. Only Veronica Fairfax lingered, wishing to speak with the sheriff, and Sr. Agnes, who was waiting on the outside porch since I'd offered to accompany her back to the orphanage.

Mrs. Fairfax was always exceedingly kind to me, even a bit solicitous, but sometimes it seemed a bit too much, and I was never quite sure what to make of it. It seemed to me that there was a gulf of sadness beneath the woman's polite gentility. I once heard the other women discussing Veronica's "change." It seems that she'd miscarried her third child eleven years ago and taken it very hard. I have no reason to believe otherwise. I realize that the death of a child, even a miscarriage, can deeply wound a woman, and I've always felt sorry for whatever she'd gone through back then and whatever she was still going through.

Regardless, as mentioned, on the surface she was always perfectly friendly and proper.

When she found herself alone with the sheriff and Annie (and me), she said, "I'd like a moment. About

Jane."

Naturally, I was flush with curiosity, and I didn't want to be forced from the room.

"Annie and Lizzie have been helping me," the sheriff explained.

She seemed to understand.

Maybe she'd heard that Annie had interviewed the vagrant boy inside his jail cell? After all, her husband was the county judge, and he probably knew what was going on.

"I feel guilty saying this," she confided, "especially since I consider Fanny one of my best friends."

I was astonished.

Veronica Fairfax was clearly on the verge of some kind of gossip, which was totally out of character. No matter what anyone says, *everybody* likes to hear a bit of gossip. Even the males of the species. But there are certain kinds of women who enjoy initiating the gossip, and certain other women who prefer to simply listen, and I'd never taken Mrs. Fairfax for the former.

"It stays with me," the sheriff assured her, "and with all of us."

She seemed reassured.

"Yesterday, I saw the mayor on Centre Bridge arguing with Jane, not very far from where she fell."

I was stunned.

"Do you have any idea," the sheriff wondered, "what they were arguing about?"

"No, I saw them from a distance, and I wondered if I should go up on the ridge and put an end to it. But then it was over, and they went their different ways."

"What time was it?"

"Around ten o'clock."

Which was about the same time she fell earlier today.

"Forgive me," Mrs. Fairfax said. "I'm sure it was nothing."

"I appreciate your honesty, Veronica."

Then, as if embarrassed, as if exposed, Mrs. Fairfax nodded politely and left immediately.

As she did so, Jimmy Granger bounded into the room looking for Miss Annie. When he saw me, he flashed his famous smile. The charming one. Jimmy's dad, the sheriff, had gotten him a job at the post office as the town courier, which was perfect for such a lively young boy like Jimmy, who could ride like the wind. He could also skate better than anyone else in town, and he was the best infielder on the Franklin Nutters, even though he was only sixteen.

We'd known each other for a long time since his father always sent him to the orphanage on Saturdays to help out and play games with the kids. He was full of life, full of mischief, full of fun. He'd also grown up to be very nice looking, and all the girls seemed to find him irresistible, but he was stuck on me. Sr. Agnes once said, "That boy's going to ask you to marry him someday," and when I laughed, she added, "Maybe you should start thinking about what you're going to say when it happens." I still had no idea about that. I was only fifteen, and I had big plans (more on that later). But I'm not about to pretend that I wasn't noticing the boys who were noticing me. Including Jimmy Granger. In the meantime, I did my best to be polite to everyone, and flirt with no one.

"Hey Liz, you look even better today than you did yesterday."

"Flattery is a character flaw," I pointed out.

"So is enjoying it."

Annie came over and rescued me.

She handed Jimmy the sealed letter.

"Are you leaving right now?"

"Yes, ma'am."

Whenever Annie and Frank were separated, they either wrote or telegrammed each other every single day. Since Frank was down in Philadelphia for the next week or so, Jimmy was riding Annie's letters down there each evening, then picking up Frank's reciprocal letter.

I hope that whenever I do find a worthwhile man to love and marry, we'll love each other like the Butlers.

"I do have a quick stop in Nutley," Jimmy remembered. "A drop-off for the judge."

Annie was curious.

"Documents?"

"I don't know," Jimmy shrugged. "I doubt it. It's a regular thing. On the twelfth of every month."

"*Every* month?"

"Yes, ma'am."

Annie, as she was prone to do, was thinking it over.

"All right, young boy, be safe."

Jimmy nodded to Annie, flashed another sneaky smile at me, then took off with her letter.

"Hmm," Annie said.

(If one can actually say a sound like Hmm.)

Naturally, I was wondering what Annie was wondering.

After all, why would someone be doing what the judge was apparently doing?

Was it a payoff of some kind?

Even though I liked the judge, I let myself ruminate. After all, I'd already decided that no one (excepting my father and Miss Annie) would be elevated "above suspicion."

So, I speculated.

In a negative fashion.

Maybe it was a bribe?

Maybe it was blackmail?

"Lizzie, my dear."

Sr. Agnes was calling me away from doing what I shouldn't be doing.

Just as she'd done so many times in the past.

"I'm coming, Sister!"

5. Cemetery

Monday, March 12, 1900

I parked my new Victoria at the edge of the cemetery.

I love Adler, of course, more than anything (who doesn't love one's horse?), but I've also come to love my bicycle, a birthday present that my father gave me this January for "quick jaunts" around town.

Which cost $100!

The Victoria is an upright step-through bicycle designed specifically for ladies and advertised as the "Queen of the Safeties." Manufactured by the Overman Wheel Company, it has durable pneumatic tires, chain drive, and a diamond steel frame.

As you might guess, Annie is a very skilled bicyclist, and, according to Mr. Frank, whom I have no reason to doubt, Annie was the first woman to ride a bicycle in London back in 1892, just before the English bicycle craze began, before it spread across the Atlantic to America.

Tonight, the night was exceptionally dark and cold, but at least the snow was mostly gone and melted. I'd had a very pleasant time accompanying Sr. Agnes back to the orphanage. She walked, as always, in her delicate, little, nun steps, and I rode alongside her, very slowly, or walked my bicycle beside her. We talked, as we always did, about many things, including dear Miss Dalton.

"I think Annie thinks it wasn't an accident," she said.

"Yes," I agreed, "but why would anyone want her dead?"

Jane Dalton, whom I learned earlier today at the sheriff's office was seventy years old, was certainly one of the most beloved women in Nutley, the dedicated "protector" of the town's library collection, which she lodged in two of the rooms in her own small house, until the town (someday!) would finally finance and build a new library.

"She knew many secrets, my dear."

Which I'd never thought about before. Aside from the books, Miss Jane also served as the keeper of the town's records, and I recalled something that she'd mentioned at Annie's last "books and tea" get-together. She was expecting a large packet of documents from the Newark library which all related to the Nutley/Franklin area.

"There are always things in our past," Sister Agnes reminded me, "that we'd like to keep buried."

"But Miss Dalton seemed to be the absolute mistress of discretion."

"She was, my dear, but the fear of exposure can be a powerful and motivating fear."

I thought it over.

"Did you mention these thoughts to Annie? Or Sheriff Granger?"

"I'm sure that Annie is well aware of the possibility. If she isn't, you can pass it along."

"I will."

"I like to keep myself out of such things."

I understood.

She had enough trouble keeping the orphanage financially afloat without getting involved in local mysteries.

Then we talked about Mr. Edison and his flickers, but mostly about the man himself.

"What surprises me the most," she said, "and delights me the most, is his complete lack of any kind of pretentiousness."

"Yes! Most of the time, I quite simply forget that he's one of the greatest geniuses on the planet! Because he's so perfectly down-to-earth. So 'regular.' Earlier tonight, he and my father were discussing, actually debating, the 'gold standard' issue in our living room, and they sounded like any other American men, huffing and puffing away about current issues."

Sr. Agnes laughed her pretty little laugh.

When we arrived at the orphanage, she took my

hand, as she always did when she wanted me to pay close attention, and she looked into my eyes.

"Be careful, my dear. Be alert."

I nodded that I would.

I watched her walk to the front door that I knew so well and enter the silent orphanage, where all the little children were asleep in their beds, just as I'd been every single night for nine years.

Then I rode my bicycle over to the cemetery, thinking about many things, especially about the dear devoted nun who'd made my orphaned life so much more than just bearable.

Exactly twelve years ago, my mother was murdered on the banks of the Passaic River. My brother as well. Early this morning, I'd gone to her grave, as I did every year, so I could "talk" to the woman I had absolutely no memory of. Not a single memory. I told her about all the events of the previous year of my life. About Adler, about my bicycle, about the boys who fancied me, including both Jimmy and Lawrence, about my father's kindness, about Annie's kindness and companionship, and much more.

But there were no flowers.

Years ago, I realized that someone was placing flowers on my mother's grave every year on the anniversary of her death. Naturally, I wondered who it was – and *why* – but I'd never been able to actually discover him or her in the act.

Since I'd seen no white lilies this morning, I was

back again tonight.

To check.

A lot of the kids at the orphanage were naturally afraid of wakes, funerals, and cemeteries. Probably because they remembered all those sorrowful things when they first became orphans. But I never felt that way, maybe because I had no memory of my mother's death, even though I was there when it happened, or maybe it was because the cemetery was the only place that I could spend time with the woman, who by all accounts loved me very much.

I made my way up the slight rise though a stand of cedars. As mentioned, it was exceedingly dark and moonless, and I had to watch my step. Suddenly I was startled. It was a rustling sound, up near my mother's headstone, and I stopped where I was, and my heart exploded, then accelerated.

So much for *not* being spooked in graveyards!

Then I noticed a vague dark figure, backing cautiously away from the tombstone, into the trees.

It was the flower person.

Surely.

The lilies were now lying at the base of the stone.

By all accounts, I'm a rather brave person, and my curiosity at the moment outweighed my fears, so I took a few steps closer and spoke to the darkness.

"I'm Elizabeth Miller."

There was a flash and sudden explosion in the darkness as a bullet shot through the night right over my head. Clearly someone with a pistol was not impressed with me.

Or with my name.

I stopped where I was.

My heart was beating dangerously fast, crashing around in my chest. Despite my overall rather excellent health, I did contract Scarlet Fever as a child, and the doctors and nuns were always overly concerned about my heart.

Maybe I should also be concerned, but tonight, I was determined to go forward.

Then another loud shot, another bullet, made me reconsider.

I called out again.

"Why do you bring flowers?"

There was no response.

Reluctantly, I turned around and returned to my Victoria, leaving whoever it was alone with my mother. I was naturally dissatisfied, and I wondered if I'd done what I should have done.

Had I been brave enough?

Then a more important problem surfaced in my mind.

Should I tell Annie?

6. Letter to Mr. Frank Butler

Monday, March 12, 1900

Dearest,

Dear Miss Jane is dead.

She fell from the high Centre Bridge over the Yantokah, as witnessed by young Lizzie. After sending her off to find the sheriff, I stood on the banks above Jane's still and lifeless form, and for some inexplicable reason, I thought of the time when you and I walked through the bizarre ruins of Pompeii at the foot of Mt. Vesuvius near the Bay of Naples. Where I stood with you, amid Pompeii's oddly preserved ruins, amid the ancient villas and shops and bathhouses, thinking about the absolute terror of the two thousand people who were completely and instantly overwhelmed and suffocated by the millions of tons of superheated volcanic ash that had spewed forth from Vesuvius. Even though it had happened over nineteen hundred years earlier, I felt completely overwhelmed with sadness and sorrow, and I cried, and you held me. Do you remember? I'm sure you do. After all, I don't cry very much. Very little in fact. But on *that* day, alone with you, amid the silent screams of the mummified remains of the dead, I was overcome.

Well, something like that happened again today, and I wish you'd been with me, to hold me. I didn't cry exactly, but I was completely overcome with sorrow for our poor dear Jane and her brutal fall into death.

Eventually, it passed, especially when I thought of you and your love.

As for the sheriff, he thinks it's an accident, but I'm not so sure.

Then something else odd happened.

The sheriff arrested a young vagrant boy, with no identification, hanging around Jane's little house, and the boy, for some reason, insisted that he'd only speak to me. When Lizzie and I went to his jail cell, I got him to talk a little bit, but not much. I realize this might seem perfectly ridiculous, but I'm wondering if he might be Ethan Miller, Lizzie's older brother? Do you remember the case? It happened about five years before we moved to Nutley.

Do you think I'm reading too much Sherlock Holmes with the other ladies?

I do hope your business is a roaring success, and I long for your return next week.

Your loving Missie

P.S. Tom came tonight with his latest contraption,

and I was forced to watch myself again, performing in his “projected” moving pictures! Fortunately, it’s only a few seconds long! Tom, as always, was wonderful. He’s off to Florida tomorrow with his family, and he made sure to insist that I send you his best.

7. Phillip

Monday, March 12, 1900

Am I a frivolous person?

I suppose I am.

I'm lying in bed, beneath my warm comforter, and I'm thinking about what I shouldn't be thinking about.

I *should*, of course, be thinking about poor Miss Jane.

Or about the strange young boy who's inexplicably materialized in our little town on the very same day that Miss Jane fell to her death.

Or about the dark and terrifying figure who fired two rounds in my direction within the darkness of the cemetery.

Or even, I suppose, about Mr. Edison's marvelous flicker machine.

But, shamefully, I wasn't thinking about any of those things, I was thinking about the handsome man who'd also entered my life on this most peculiar day.

I was now fantasizing:

I imagined the two of us, dressed in "all the fashions," dining at an elegant restaurant in New York City. (Even though I've never been across the Hudson.)

Then walking the fashionable promenade at Elysian Fields in Hoboken. (As I was carrying a marvelous, white-lace parasol to match my dress.)

Then entering Gracie Mansion for the Mayor's Ball in Manhattan. (The band was playing "I Dream of Jeannie with the Light Brown Hair.")

Then perusing valuable manuscripts in the archives of the Newark Public Library.

"Look at this, my dear Lizzie," he said, "a letter written by Mr. Thackeray to his wife, Isabella."

Then lots more similar nonsense, but I must admit, I was enjoying myself.

Within the confines of these childish fantasies, Mr. Phillip Palmer was dressed much as he was earlier today, in a perfectly tailored gray suit, with a high-collared white shirt, black tie, and a gold watch and chain.

Maybe these attractions, these infatuations, were the reason (I suddenly realized) that I'd almost left my newly appointed tutor off my "suspect" list.

After all, he'd entered into our lives just a few hours after poor Miss Jane fell to her death.

Or maybe I believed that he was too handsome to be involved?

Too handsome to be a murderer?

Had I really considered excusing him on the

shallow grounds of his dashing good looks?

His charms?

Rather than respond (mentally) to my own uncomfortable interrogatives, I imagined myself dancing a lovely waltz in the arms of my attentive companion.

Smiling all the while, having the most wonderful time.

I hope you might believe me when I assure you that this kind of girlish behavior was definitely not a regular nighttime habit. It's true that, on occasion, I did reflect rather fondly on either one of my two local "beaus," as Miss Annie calls them, before I drifted off to peaceful sleep.

My young Jimmy.

My brave deputy, Lawrence.

Both of whom, in their own very different ways, had been pursuing me for years.

But this was different.

Very different.

It was both wonderful and disturbing.

Was it some kind of silly "crush"?

Was I really that pathetic?

That trite, that commonplace, that ordinary?

Looking back at this afternoon, I'm perfectly willing to admit that Phillip Palmer's behavior towards me, although exceedingly polite and respectful, never indicated anything more than that. There was nothing "telling" in his soft dark eyes. Then again, what would one expect? After all, he was sitting amid strangers, within the careful scrutiny of a distinguished medical doctor, my father, supplicating for a teaching position.

As for me, whatever his interest or disinterest might be, I would suggest in my own defense that very few unattached fifteen-year-old girls would have witnessed such a handsome and dignified young man enter into their sphere without some kind of attraction.

I remembered what Jane Austen's Darcy said in *Pride and Prejudice*:

> *A lady's imagination is very rapid; it jumps from admiration to love, from love to matrimony in a moment.*

Well, I'll admit it, I was definitely being a bit too "rapid," *much* too "rapid," but I certainly wasn't about to make any subsequent "jumps."

Certainly not to "love."

Of course not.

And certainly not to thoughts of "marriage."

How ridiculous.

It was just a young girl's fantasies.

Her charming rather absurdist images of being escorted throughout polite society by a very handsome and most solicitous young man.

After all, could I really love a man who preferred the novels of someone named Cantell Bigly to William Makepeace Thackeray?

Although, to be perfectly honest, it's most probable that neither Jimmy nor Lawrence could have identified either author.

Finally, I fell off to sleep.

I believe, at that moment, Mr. Palmer was offering me a selection from a tray of delicious tortes.

Smiling.

8. Me

Tuesday, March 13, 1900

Since you all know about Annie Oakley, I suppose I should tell you a little bit about "nobody from nowhere."

Meaning me.

Annie's "Watson."

Her Boswell.

(Please do me a kindness and forget about last night's nocturnal ruminations.)

As you know by now, I'm fifteen years old, unmarried, and I've spent much of my life as an orphan. My father, by all accounts, a decent, loving, hardworking man, died in a work accident at a nearby quarry eight months before I was born. When I was three years old, my mother was murdered, along with my older brother, and the very same day I was taken to St. Mary's Orphanage. The nuns and the staff were exceedingly kind, doing their best to comfort me, but Sr. Agnes Marie took a special interest. Overall, I was well-treated, well-educated, and I had many wonderful friends. In truth, I suffered far far less than so many other orphans in this difficult world.

Now (if I'm to be perfectly honest) I would have to admit that I was both rather athletic and rather bright. Sr. Agnes once described me as "precocious," which upset me at the time, since I thought the word was a synonym for "rambunctious."

In some ways, I suppose I was both.

I won all the academic writing awards, as well as the spelling and history awards. Fortunately, the other kids never seemed jealous about it, as if it was taken for granted. Then, seven years ago, my life changed.

Irrevocably.

Annie Oakley and Frank Butler moved to Nutley.

The first time I saw Annie Oakley, she was standing on a horse in an apple field demolishing targets with her Marlin '91.

Yes! Standing!

Yes! The horse was moving!

Then a month later she came to the orphanage to entertain the children with riding and shooting tricks, and we were all perfectly mesmerized. At one point, as she was shooting targets set a hundred feet behind her, using a mirror, little Jeanie Wilson cried out. She was sitting near the edge of the grass and looking down in horror at a quite agitated Copperhead snake, whose ugly poisonous head was a few inches away from Jeanie's pretty face, and seemingly ready to strike.

Everyone, including the nuns, gasped in horror. As I rose up, intending to grab the child and pull her away from the ugly creature, the snake's head exploded from a dead shot .22 caliber cartridge.

That was the end of that problem.

Later, Sr. Agnes made a point of introducing me to Annie, and she quickly became my friend and protector. Annie had grown up very poor in western Ohio, essentially fatherless, and she'd once worked at an infirmary full of orphans. As a result, she's always done benefit performances for orphans, both here and abroad. Since Annie and Frank were childless, she'd developed special relationships with several of her nieces, especially Fern Campbell, and also with some of her co-workers' children, especially Johnny Baker's little daughters, Gladys and Della.

Now me.

She taught me to ride, to shoot, and to sew, and she always encouraged the books. In her own youth, she was too poor to attend normal schooling, so she was essentially self-taught, and a great proponent of serious education.

Then tragedy struck.

Mrs. Miriam Carlyle, Annie's close friend and next-door neighbor, took a bad fever three years ago and died unexpectedly and suddenly. Dr. Carlyle took it very hard, but after several months, he grew tired of his empty home, and Annie encouraged him to adopt a child.

Me!

Which he did.

Yes, it's true, I was an orphan, but I was also the luckiest of them all, having Sr. Agnes, Annie, and now Dr. Carlyle in my life.

In a sense of fair disclosure, I should now mention several of my own personal failings, and I hope you'll permit me to mention only a few, which might assist you in your overall appraisal of my character.

Vanity.

Ah, yes, vanity!

I'm rather pretty, although no particular credit is due on my part. Sister Agnes seemed to recognize the problem quite early on, and she wrote "All is Vanity" from Ecclesiastes across the top of my personal looking glass when I was a young child, and I still use the same glass every morning in my bedroom at the Carlyle house. Whenever I look in the mirror, below the inscription, I see the lush, sometimes hard to manage, dark brown hair, deep dark eyes, with contrasting and perfectly clear light complexion, and unkissed lips. The good sisters taught me to walk like a lady, and Annie has taught me to run and ride like a lady.

I'm five foot five inches, thus five full inches taller than Annie Oakley. Even though we never had much in the way of clothing at the orphanage, I definitely like clothes, especially pretty dresses, although nothing showy or ostentatious, just pretty and/or practical dresses depending on the occasion.

So what do I want to do with my life?

There was never any question. I fully intend, if heaven permits, to become a nurse and comfort the sick. At present, living with a distinguished doctor, he's been instructing me as a nurse-in-training and sometimes taking me on his rounds. Next year, I plan to go to college. Unfortunately, there's no ladies college at Rutgers, so I plan to go to Bryn Mawr, which is not too far away in Pennsylvania. Despite my age, I've already been accepted for the coming fall. The school's motto is *Veritatem Dilexi*, meaning "I Delight in the Truth," which I definitely intend to do, and I also have hopes, eventually, to create a new kind of specialty. What Dr. Carlyle and I refer to as "ladies health," with a focus on sports activities for women, including riding, athletics, and hunting. After all, keeping people from getting sick is yet another way to care for the sick.

Annie Oakley, of course, is the world's most important proponent of outdoor activities for women, believing that it improves both their overall well-being and their family life, and I'd like to find a way to promote it as well, from a nursing perspective.

I hope my ambitions don't seem like further examples of my multifarious vanities.

As for men, well, my dark eyes are wide open!

What else do I have to report?

I love baseball, of course, especially Mr. George Davis, outfielder for my hapless New York Giants. I also love riding, running, cycling, sewing, and reading.

I love Annie's toasted muffins and jelly cakes. I love Jane Austen, Edgar Allan Poe, Charlotte Brontë, Jules Verne, Mr. Dickens, Mr. Thackeray, Frank Stockton, and (does it show?) I've recently gotten hooked on Sherlock Holmes at Annie's "books and tea" get-togethers. I've also kept an extensive scrapbook about the career of Annie Oakley ever since I was eight years old, the year before she moved to Nutley.

In summary, I'm not ashamed to say:

I love my life!

9. Library

Tuesday, March 13, 1900

The woman that Sherlock Holmes most admired was from New Jersey.

Of course!

> *To Sherlock Holmes she is always* the *woman. I have seldom heard him mention her under any other name. In his eyes she eclipses and predominates the whole of her sex.*

Well, I wouldn't go that far, after all, in spite of her significant operatic accomplishments, Irene Adler was a rather sketchy woman, an "adventuress," as Dr. Watson describes her, but I have to admit, I certainly appreciate the New Jersey angle.

So did the Nutley ladies when we discussed it at Annie's "books and tea" several Sundays ago. We were reading, or rereading, the twelve detection tales in *The Adventures of Sherlock Holmes*, published by Harper

Brothers a few years back.

"It's interesting," remarked Miss Jane, now deceased, "that the very first of the stories is about a woman from New Jersey who actually outwits the almost impossible-to-outwit consulting detective."

"Yes," agreed Fanny Langley, "and what's that ironic line in the story from Dr. Watson?"

She thumbed through a few pages and read the line out loud:

> *So accustomed was I to his invariable success that the very possibility of his failing had ceased to enter into my head.*

Even Mr. Holmes could be outwitted.

A good lesson for us all.

"Well," Mrs. Fairfax cautioned, "maybe we shouldn't be so pleased with ourselves, ladies. It's true that she sang at La Scala, but she's also a loose woman and a cunning blackmailer."

"Yes," agreed Theresa Morning Dove, who seldom said much of anything, "but she was treated badly by the King of Bohemia."

Which no one disputed.

"I suspect," Annie suspected, "that she was modeled on Lola Montez," who was the rather notorious mistress of King Ludwig I of Bavaria, the father of nutty Ludwig.

"Or maybe even," Miss Jane suggested, "Lillie

Langtry, who was well-known as the 'Jersey Lily.'"

Who was, herself, a famous performer and royal mistress.

So my head was full of Sherlock Holmes, and his stories, and his crimes, and his solutions, when poor Miss Jane fell to her death from the bridge, as I dismounted from my horse Adler, who was actually named last year for the New Jersey adventuress when I first read "A Scandal in Bohemia." Then Miss Annie rode up behind me, commenting on the open wound on Rusty's head, and I thought to myself, "Am I, at the present moment, standing in the midst of a mystery?"

Believing that it might be probable, I determined to become just like Dr. Watson and write everything down, everything relative, before I went to sleep each night.

Like Dr. Watson, doing my best to keep to my subservient observatory role.

"How are you doing, dear?" Annie asked.

It was her polite way of terminating my reverie and bringing me back to the task at hand.

"No longer distracted," I assured her, and she smiled her lovely smile.

We were sitting in the house of the dead. In the comfortable little house of the late Jane Dalton, in one of the two rooms she reserved for the town's library collection and legal records. We were, at the moment, reading the new documents that had recently arrived from the Newark Library. It was a sizeable pile, and we were burrowing through multifarious property archives; birth, baptism, and marriage certificates; incorporation registers; and various other rather boring legal documents.

Which was why my mind had wandered.

I immediately determined to press forward again, which I did for at least another hour or so until I was shocked to discover the name of my mother, Rebecca Miller, in a record of her last will and testament from thirteen years ago.

"I've come across my mother," I said out loud.

Annie put down her own documents and waited.

"It's a record of her last will and testament, and the executor was Owen Fairfax."

Which surprised us both.

That was back before Judge Fairfax had become the county judge, when, apparently, as a civil attorney, he'd executed my mother's will. Although Judge Fairfax was an exceedingly busy man, I'd met him a number of times over the years. He was always polite and courteous, but he'd never mentioned my mother.

Never.

Not once.

Neither did his wife, Veronica.

"Did you know that the judge had a relationship with your mother?"

"No," I said, shaking my head. "I had no idea."

But Miss Jane, before tumbling to her death, most probably did.

"How much do you know about your mother's death, Lizzie?"

When I shrugged, Annie nodded, as if to say, "Maybe it's about time."

But she said nothing, so I decided to be patient.

"Have *you* found anything of interest?" I wondered.

"Not really," Annie admitted, "just a surprise. Lawrence Langley wasn't born in Manasquan."

Everyone in town knew that the mayor and his wife Fanny had grown up in Manasquan, married there, and moved to Nutley after the birth of their son, Lawrence.

"Where was he born?"

"In New Castle."

I'd never heard of it.

"Where is it?"

"Western Pennsylvania."

Like Annie, I was surprised. It seems that my handsome deputy had been born in the Quaker State.

"Let's finish things, Lizzie," Annie suggested, which we did rather efficiently with no more surprises.

At Annie's suggestion, we walked to my house in the fading twilight. After what had happened the previous night, Annie was armed. She was determined to protect me.

She was carrying a pistol in her handbag.

"What is it?" I asked.

She knew what I meant.

"My Stevens Gould."
I knew it well:

.22 caliber, J. Stevens Arms, 1892, single-shot pistol, Model: Gould #37, iron frame, nickeled, blued octagon barrel, fine bore, adjustable rear site, handsome walnut grips.

When we arrived at my house, we went straight to my bedroom. Annie wanted to see my mementos, so I removed the little wooden box from beneath my bed, and we looked at the few surviving keepsakes that remained of the life of my murdered mother. There was a small embroidered purse, a white opal ring and necklace (both of which matched the opal bracelet I was wearing, which I wore every single day), and three photos.

The fourth photo was on the wall next to my bed, near a framed picture of Annie herself, holding her Marlin '91, and a newspaper photo of George Davis looking quite handsome in his New York Giants uniform.

Carefully, Annie examined the remnants of my mother's short life especially the three photos:

The one of my mother, looking remarkably beautiful and happy in the whites of her wedding day.

> *The one, shot from behind, of my mother and my father standing at the altar professing their vows.*
>
> *And the one of a cute little toddler in an adorable sailor's outfit, who was clearly my older brother, Ethan, whom I'd also lost on the day of my mother's murder.*

"He has a bandage on his forearm," she said, almost to herself.

I looked closer. She was definitely correct, although I had no idea what it could possibly mean.

Annie looked into my eyes.

Her own eyes were a soft blue-gray and lovely.

"I'd like you to wear your mother's opal ring tomorrow."

"Of course."

I had my suspicions why, but I was doing my best to heed the advice of Mr. Sherlock Holmes in the Irene Adler story:

> *It is a capital mistake to theorize before one has data. Insensibly one begins to twist facts to suit theories, instead of theories to suit facts.*

10. Oedipus

Tuesday, March 13, 1900

Who killed the king of Thebes?

That's a problem for Oedipus to figure out.

Did he have a choice in the matter?

That's a problem for *all* of us to figure out.

I was sitting at the dining room table across from my new professor, discussing our first classics lesson.

Much like yesterday, Mr. Palmer was wearing expensively well-tailored clothing, a classically cut suit with an impeccably starched white shirt and gold cufflinks. He was, as previously, just as handsome as were his clothes, and he was also quite knowledgeable about Sophocles, although he badly mispronounced several Greek names, especially *Iokástē (*Jocasta). I fully realize that there are a number of acceptable variants, and I fear to be characterized as a pronunciation snob, but Sr. Agnes was always extremely exacting about both her Greek and her Latin, and she tried to make me equally conscientious.

Mr. Palmer had chosen *Oedipus Tyrannus*, a mystery, as our first lesson together, which seemed quite appropriate.

I may be only fifteen years old, and I should, as the good sisters had taught me, be hesitant about making grand and sweeping declarations, but it seems to me that *Oedipus* is quite simply the greatest mystery ever conceived. I'll readily admit that I haven't read *all* of the mysteries ever recorded or concocted, but given the play's peculiar resolution, I suspect that it would be virtually impossible to conjure a more stupefying mystery.

Yes, the story is gruesomely sensationalized – with prophesies, thwarted infanticide, a bloodthirsty monster, a ridiculous riddle, multiple murders, patricide, a devastating plague, incest, suicide by hanging, self-blinding, etc. – but it's also the greatest mystery ever plotted, which seems to be fully supported by Aristotle in the *Poetics*.

As part of my previous education, I'd read all three of the Theban tragedies numerous times, so today's discussions with Mr. Palmer were, in truth, rather effortless. Normally, I might have been distracted (as I was last night in my warm bed) by such a charming and pleasant young man sitting directly across from me, showing such an earnest concern for my intellectual development. Or, maybe, I might have been distracted by wandering thoughts about tomorrow night's Valentine's Dance. But, in truth, I was much more distracted by my own present entanglement in the mystery regarding the possible murder of Miss Jane Dalton.

Not the bloodied death of Laius, King of Thebes.

"Do you think, Elizabeth, that he had a choice?" Mr. Palmer wondered, pulling me back to Thebes and asking the two-thousand-year-old question:

Meaning: Are the prophesies of the oracle deterministic?

Or did Oedipus have the capacity to do otherwise?

Meaning free will.

Free choice.

"The reason that Oedipus behaves as he does," I pontificated, "being symbolically 'blinded' before his actual blinding, is the consequence of his terrible and often petty vanity. His pride. *Tyrannus*."

I hoped I didn't sound too cocksure, too arrogant, too vain.

Palmer seemed pleased.

"Tell me more."

I continued my huffs and puffs.

"Just because God, in his providence, knows what I'll be doing later this evening, that in no way inhibits my free will in the present moment."

I wasn't very happy with the way I'd attempted to express myself, but, again, he seemed perfectly pleased.

I knew next to nothing of the man's personal past, but I suspected that he'd been forced to make some hard choices in his own life, and that he felt that his choices were very much his own.

Not a matter of some kind of inevitability.

"Excellent," he decided. "Why don't we leave the Greeks right where they are?"

Which meant that lesson number one was over.

"We'll look at *Colonus* tomorrow."

Which was fine with me.

Then my father entered the room.

"We have guests, my dear."

He was soon followed by Annie and Sheriff Granger. After the adults had exchanged polite salutations with Mr. Palmer, my tutor left the room with Sophocles in hand.

There was, I noticed, a certain somberness in the air.

A kind of adult seriousness.

"Let's retreat to the living room," my father suggested.

We did so, with Annie and I sitting on the couch, my father settling into his usual chair, and the sheriff pulling up a chair close to the couch right in front of me.

In an intimate, not-at-all intimidating, manner.

But he seemed hesitant, something which was rare in both his demeanor and his character.

"Your father and Miss Annie have asked me to tell you about the death of your mother."

I was surprised, but not taken aback. I'd often wondered about the details, and I suppose it was time.

"Are you amenable, Lizzie?" my father asked with concern. "The details are rather unpleasant."

"I would like to know," I assured them all, and I looked over at Annie. "And I'm very grateful."

When she nodded, Sheriff Granger told me what he remembered about that day, twelve years ago, when he was still a deputy sheriff and the first person to arrive at the riverbank.

"Your mother, as you know, was a widow at the time. I didn't know her very well, but from all accounts she was a lovely person, a dedicated mother. That afternoon, as she did most afternoons, she took a walk with her children alongside the river. Ethan was five years old at the time, and you were three. At some point, your mother was shot three times in the back and died, I'm sure, instantly. When she fell to the ground, she was robbed of the few possessions she was carrying.

"When I arrived at the scene, you were sitting on top of your mother humming a little song. You seemed to think that your mother was sleeping. As for Ethan, he was nowhere to be found, and we assumed that he'd probably tried to defend your mother and was similarly killed. Possibly shot. Possibly strangled. Possibly thrown into the flowing river, although his body was never found. We searched as well as we could, finding, three days later, a purse, a ring, and a necklace wrapped in an old handkerchief on the banks of the river."

"I'm aware," I asked, "that my mother's jewelry

wasn't very valuable, but why would they abandon it?"

"I have no idea," the sheriff admitted. "Maybe your mother had something else in her possession that day that was more highly valued."

"Or maybe," Annie added, "it wasn't a robbery."

The sheriff shrugged, then continued.

"As far as we could tell, your mother had no enemies, but, of course, people commit murders for all kinds of reasons. Like anger, jealousy, or even vengeance."

I didn't know what to say. It was hard not to think about the beautiful woman in my photographs, whom I had no memory of, being brutally shot in the back and bleeding to death.

"What song?" Annie asked the sheriff.

He tried to remember.

"Something popular, but I can't remember."

Annie turned to my father.

"Were you called to the scene, Matt?"

"No, I was out of town that day, so Dr. Erickson went down to the riverside. He was my mentor back in the day."

"Now deceased?"

"Yes."

"Who was his nurse?"

"Vivian Wright. She also worked for me for a while before she retired."

"Is she still in town?"

"Yes. At her family home on Highfield Lane."

There was a knock on the outside door, and Jimmy walked into the room unannounced, as was not uncommon, but he seemed much more serious this evening.

"Forgive me for interrupting, Dr. Carlyle, but there's a pressing telegram."

He handed the telegram to my father, who read it quickly, then looked at the rest of us.

"There's been a train derailment in Newark. It sounds quite serious, and my colleagues at St. Michael's have asked me to come and help. I'll be leaving right away."

The sheriff thought it over. As we all knew, his cousin was now a captain in the Newark Police force.

"I'll leave early tomorrow morning."

"I'd like to help," Annie offered. Her mother had once been a part-time frontier nurse, and Annie had developed considerable nursing skills on tour with Buffalo Bill's Wild West Show.

My father rose from his chair and looked at Annie.

"Is Lizzie in any danger?"

Which was rather surprising.

I'd told Annie, of course, about the incident at the cemetery last night, but I'd downplayed it enough that Annie agreed, "for the moment, at least," that we'd keep it to ourselves.

Maybe it was just a father's inexplicable sense of danger involving his daughter.

Annie, as always, was truthful.

"I think she might be, Matthew."

"Then maybe I should bring her to Newark?" he said, as if asking himself.

We all waited.

I would have been glad to help anyone I could in Newark, but I also very much wanted to stay in Nutley and help Annie figure out what had happened to Jane Dalton.

Finally, my father looked over at Annie.

"Could Lizzie stay with you while I'm gone?"

A few years ago, Mr. Frank had mentioned in passing that Annie had never shot another "human being," and that she hoped that she would never need to, but if any of her friends or relatives were ever in danger, she'd certainly be ready to do whatever she needed to do.

It was clear that my father was putting me in the care of the best "marksman" in the entire world.

She didn't hesitate.

"Of course."

She looked at the sheriff.

"Can I snoop around while you're gone?"

We all knew what that meant.

"You can do whatever you like, Annie."

"Whatever?"

"Whatever."

I was delighted.

"I'll get you a badge," he added.

I wondered if Annie was the first and only woman

in America to be deputized. Then I wondered if maybe it had happened before.

Right here in Nutley.

11. Morning Dove

Tuesday, March 13, 1900

I was sitting on the couch in Annie's dark-paneled "sportsman's room," surrounded by her countless trophies, awards, citations, and, of course, the numerous racks and displays of her many rifles, shotguns, and handguns.

Nearby, Theresa Morning Dove sat in a small black-leather chair, and we did what we usually did under similar circumstances, we sat in silence. It wasn't the slightest bit awkward or uncomfortable, just a bit peculiar. Theresa was always kind and polite and thoughtful, and I'd come to believe that her chronic taciturnity was just a natural aspect of her personality and not the result, at least in Annie's home, of feeling somehow out of place, feeling somehow geographically or culturally disjointed.

Theresa Morning Dove had been born and raised on the Pine Ridge Indian Reservation in South Dakota. A "Hunkpapa" Lakota, her grandfather was Sitting

Bull, who'd inspired a powerful confederation of Lakota with Northern Cheyennes to decimate the Seventh Cavalry under Lt. Col. George Armstrong Custer in 1876. 268 U.S. soldiers died at Little Bighorn that day, and Sitting Bull, overnight, became world famous. He also became the most hunted man in the United States, so he retreated into Canada before eventually surrendering and returning to the Dakotas and the Standing Rock Agency.

In 1884, he was allowed to go "on tour," mostly in the northern states, as curious Americans flocked to see the famous Lakota warrior. In 1884, in Minnesota, he attended a performance by a young sharpshooter named Annie Oakley. Astonished by her skills and believing that she had supernatural powers, he "adopted" her after the show and gave her the name *Watanya Cicilla*, meaning "Little Sure Shot." They immediately became fast friends, later performing together in Colonel Cody's incredibly popular Wild West Show.

Americans (including me!) love everything about our fading Western frontier: its history, the gunfights, the pony express, the wagon trains, the Indian raids, and all the shooting-roping-and-riding. But things had ended badly for Sitting Bull. Back home on the reservation in 1889, he got involved with the Paiute Ghost Dance Movement, apparently instigating an uprising, and was killed the following year when he refused to be arrested. In the ensuing shootout, eight federal officers, several of whom were Indian, as well as seven of Sitting Bull's followers, were killed.

That was ten years ago.

When her famous grandfather died, Theresa Morning Dove was nine years old, but she still had many tender memories of a loving grandfather. On those rare occasions when we actually did talk, I would always encourage her to tell me stories about Annie's "adoptive" father, and she did so with both fondness and good humor.

Mostly, however, we sat together in silence.

I would often wonder if, like me, she was thinking about the silence between us, or if, to her, it seemed perfectly normal and natural.

I had no idea.

Then she spoke.

Unexpectedly.

She was wearing a lovely, green, gingham house dress with beautiful leather moccasins, which I believe she'd made herself. As mentioned earlier, Theresa was remarkably beautiful, with charcoal eyes and long jet-black hair that tumbled over her shoulders then midway down her back.

"Have you ever been in love?"

I was taken aback by her question. By its intimacy. I also wasn't sure if I knew the answer to her question, but I did my best.

"I don't think so, Theresa," I tried to explain. "Not *true* love. Not yet, anyway. I've certainly had my attractions, even infatuations and urges, but never anything like a marrying kind of love."

I wondered if the word "urges" sounded a bit crude, but she seemed to understand perfectly.

When she didn't respond, I felt it appropriate to turn the tables.

"Have you?"

"Yes."

There was no hesitation, but it was also clear that if I wanted more details, I'd have to work a bit harder.

"Could you tell me more?"

She thought it over.

"It's quite terrifying," she admitted. "I had no idea. I was struck like a flash of lightning, and everything within me changed forever. It was perfectly devastating. Perfectly wonderful and beautiful."

I was amazed by her intensity, and I wanted more.

"Was it reciprocal?"

She smiled.

Theresa's smiles are rare, very beautiful, very heart crushing.

"Yes."

"Could you tell me more?"

Annie came into the room.

It was the one-and-only time in my life when I wished Annie wasn't there.

"I wish that I could," Theresa said, and I believed her.

Annie looked down at both of us, at her two "young girls," and she smiled.

"Why do I have the feeling that you two have been discussing the male of the species?"

I laughed.

"We were talking about George Davis," I kidded, referring to my baseball "crush."

"Of course, you were," Annie said knowingly, as she went to one of her racks and took down her favorite Marlin '91. "Let's go snooping."

It was now evening, rather lovely for March, as the two of us walked down the quiet tree-lined streets of Nutley to the Wright home on Highfield Lane. A young girl answered the door, and she was very pleased to see Annie Oakley standing on her front porch. After Annie left her Marlin safely inside the front door, the young girl led us upstairs to the bedroom of the elderly Miss Deborah Norris.

The retired nurse seemed to be somewhere in her mid-eighties, in debilitated health, but with high and contagious spirits, as she lay beneath an exquisite white quilt in her small wooden bed.

"Just what I need," she decided happily, "lady visitors!"

I liked her immediately, and it was clear that Annie did as well. The old woman asked about my father, Dr. Carlyle, and about the death of Miss Dalton. Then she continued with a series of questions about Annie's various seasons abroad with the Wild West Show.

"I read somewhere that the King of Senegal wanted to purchase you for a hundred thousand francs?"

"Yes," Annie remembered. "It's true. It was at the Exposition in Paris. Fortunately, Colonel Cody made it perfectly clear that I wasn't for sale."

"What did he want?"

"He wanted me to shoot renegade tigers. It seems that several jungle tigers had been terrorizing rural villages."

I knew the rest of the story.

Mr. Frank once told me that when the king realized that he wouldn't be able to "purchase" Miss Annie, he dropped down to his knees in respect, kissed her hand, and then rose like royalty and left the room.

It's certainly a strange world out there.

Eventually, our bedridden host looked over at Annie.

"I suspect you've come with a purpose."

It was time to get down to business.

"Yes," Annie explained, "I'd like to ask you some questions about Rebecca Miller."

The old woman looked over at me.

"Your lovely mother, my dear," she said, and I nodded with appreciation, as Annie continued.

"Were you there the day her body was found?"

"Yes," she remembered. "The scene was first discovered by Mr. Granger, who was a deputy back then, and Dr. Erickson was called to the scene. At the time, we were making rounds together, and when the message arrived, we took his carriage to the riverbank."

"What do you remember?"

"I remember being horrified," she said, looking at me again. "Your mother was dead on the ground, your brother was missing, and you were sitting next to your mother. Actually, you were sitting *on top of* your mother, seemingly unaware of what had happened, humming a little song."

"What song?" Annie asked.

"I'm sorry, I can't remember. I'm sure I was in shock at the time. Nurses deal with all kinds of injury, disease, and death, but the murder of your dear mother, shot in the back, was something I'll never forget."

"Did you know Rebecca?"

"Not really. Just a few polite 'hellos' around town, and a few visits to her home when the children had the croup. I was, of course, fully aware of her reputation as a charming woman, struggling to maintain her two young children after the tragic death of her husband."

Annie produced one of the photos.

"Could you look at this?"

She handed the photo to Miss Wright who examined it closely.

Then smiling.

"Yes, that's little Ethan, God bless his soul. He was such a lively sweet little boy."

"He has a dressing on his forearm," Annie pointed out. "Did you treat the wound?"

"I did. Dr. Erickson sent me over to the house that day. It was a burn. I believe it was caused by a flash fire in the kitchen. The little boy was very brave, and I remember showing Rebecca how to apply the ointment and change the bandages."

"Was it bad?"

"It wasn't good, but you know how children are. I'm sure he was over it in a few weeks or so."

Annie now knew what she wanted to know.

After a few more pleasantries, we left the woman's bedroom, exited the house, and, as planned, headed for the sheriff's office.

I believed I knew why.

12. Jail

Tuesday, March 13, 1900

Annie stood at the sheriff's desk, carefully examining the shell casings. She was, of course, an expert about such things.

A world-class expert.

The three casings were all that remained of the murder investigation from twelve years ago, except for Sheriff Granger's crime report, which Annie had just read, and which I was currently perusing. It was a succinct account of what I'd already been told by the sheriff, but I did learn that my mother, when her body was found, was still wearing her opal bracelet. The one that I still wear every single day in her memory. As to "why" the bracelet had not been stolen along with her purse, her ring, and her necklace, I had no idea.

Neither did Sheriff Granger.

I also learned that my mother's mother's name was Clementina. My grandmother had apparently lived in neighboring Belleview, but she'd died several years before the murder took place.

Annie put the casings back in a little box and looked at the sheriff.

"They're Czech. Sellier & Bellot casings for a 12-guage shotgun."

"Are they rare?"

"Somewhat. At least, here in the States. They were quite popular for a while in Germany and France."

"I'm glad I kept them."

"Why did you?"

He shrugged.

"I don't really know. They looked odd to me, so I saved them."

"It was a smart thing to do so."

When I finished reading the report, I looked up.

"Are you ready, my dear?" Annie asked.

"Yes."

"Do you understand my suspicions?"

"I believe I do."

"It would be best if the sheriff knows before we go into the next room."

So, I assumed that Annie wanted me to elucidate for the sheriff.

"I believe," I explained, "that Miss Annie believes that the motive for the murder wasn't robbery, but rather abduction."

He seemed stunned by the idea, but he quickly put things together.

"To kidnap your brother?"

"Yes."

"Whom I believe," Annie explained, "is sitting in the next room."

Meaning the jail cell.

Now the sheriff was even more stunned, and I fully expected him to say, "That's ridiculous!" or something like that, but he didn't. He just looked at Miss Annie and said rather calmly:

"Well, I doubt that, Annie."

"I understand," she said. "Let's go into the next room and find out."

Always the gentleman, the sheriff held open the door, and we entered the adjacent room. This time the young boy was standing in the center of his cell looking up, rather forlornly, at one of the high windows in his small cell. When he heard us enter, he immediately sat down on his little bench, just as he had yesterday, and stared down at the floor.

When the sheriff opened the cell door, we entered, but this time Annie sat down on the small wooden bench right next to the prisoner.

"Are you all right, young man?"

"I'm fine."

He wasn't convincing.

"I want you to know that we're all aware that you're Ethan Miller."

He looked at Miss Annie.

Expressionless.

"You're mistaken about that, ma'am," he said

politely. "I have no idea who that might be."

Annie ignored him, nodding at me.

"This young woman is your younger sister, Elizabeth Miller."

He refused to look at me directly.

"The reason that you're staring at her hands is that you remember your mother's opal jewelry. Her bracelet and her ring."

He looked away from my hands.

"Are you familiar with the song, 'Oh My Darling, Clementine'?"

He shook his head "no," but the sheriff butted in.

"I've heard you humming that song more than once, boy. It was definitely 'Clementine.'"

The boy shrugged.

"For many years," Annie explained, "I've worked with a Wild West show, and I've heard that song sung many times, in many different variations. Some of the men who worked on the show had gone, in their youths, to California and prospected during the Gold Rush. It's a very pretty song that began as a sentimental love song, a tragic lament, but ended up a humorous parody of itself."

Annie began to sing.

I was astonished. We all were.

She has a pretty soprano, soft and lovely.

Drove she ducklings to the water
Ev'ry morning just at nine,

Hit her foot against a splinter,
Fell into the foaming . . ."

She waited for Ethan.

"Brine," he said.

"Yes," Annie continued, "I believe your mother sang that song around the house, and maybe her own mother had done the same. Did you know that your grandmother's name was Clementina?"

The boy said nothing, still trying to resist.

"Give me your left hand."

The boy, obviously confused, did as he was told.

Annie slid up the left sleeve of his blue-green flannel shirt, and I could see the burn. The scar was about three inches long, no longer discolored, and not very noticeable unless you were paying close attention.

"When you were a young boy, you burned yourself in the kitchen. Earlier tonight, your sister and I spoke to the nurse who first tended your wound."

Annie handed him the photo of a happy little boy with a bandage on his arm.

"That's you, Ethan, before you were abducted and before your mother was killed."

The boy made no response, emotionally or otherwise, but his defenses were down.

"Tell us about it," Annie encouraged.

He tried.

"I really don't remember that day, and I don't remember my mother at all, although the name

'Rebecca' seems familiar. I'm afraid I don't remember much of anything."

"Tell me what you *do* remember."

He shrugged.

"I spent much of my youth in a lightly lit room. Inside a storage barn. And I never went outside, but I was well-fed and well taken care of."

"How long did it last?"

"About five years."

"Can you read, Ethan?"

He seemed ashamed.

"Not really."

"It's not your fault."

When Ethan didn't respond, Annie continued.

"Then what happened?"

"I was allowed to work around the farm with my father, which I enjoyed very much."

"Who else was on the farm?"

"No one, just me and my parents."

"What are their names?"

He hesitated.

"I never knew their last name, but my father's name was Silas, and my mother's name was Virginia."

It seemed to me that he was lying. Trying to protect his "parents."

"Where did you live?"

"New York. In an upstate farming region."

"What town?"

"I don't know."

"Describe the surrounding area?"

"I only saw the farm."

He tried to picture it in his mind.

"We had about twenty acres, with a storage barn and a nice log cabin. There was a narrow river, more like a wide stream, that ran through the northwest corner of the property, and off in the distant west, there were high gray mountains, one higher than the rest."

"Did the stream have a name? Or the mountains?"

"Not to me, they were just 'the river' and 'the mountains.'"

"Were the 300 Steps nearby?"

"I don't know. My father mentioned them once or twice, but I never saw them."

"Did you live in the house?"

"No, I always stayed in my room in the barn."

"Then what happened, Ethan? How did you end up here?"

"I don't know what happened."

He seemed genuinely confused and conflicted, but he did his best to explain what seemed to him inexplicable.

"One day my father took me away in his carriage. It was a very long drive, over twelve hours, and he dropped me off at a train station called Albany, with a ticket for New York City and some traveling money. I didn't want to leave, but I had no choice. I also had no idea where I was going or what I was supposed to be doing. While sitting on the train, I remembered the name of a place that my mother had mentioned a number of times. It was an odd name. 'Nutley.'

"Eventually, after some confusion about whether the town was called Franklin or Nutley, I purchased another train ticket in New York City for Nutley, New Jersey. When I arrived, I immediately went to the supply store to try to get some information, and I was told that either the sheriff or the town librarian might be able to help me. So I tried to find the librarian. Miss Dalton. But I never did."

"Is that where you heard someone mention my name?"

"Yes, they seemed eager to tell an outsider like me that you lived here. So I figured you were famous."

"But you had no idea why?"

"No. But I've learned this morning that you're very good with a gun."

It was hard not to smile.

"What kind of crops did you grow on the farm?"

Annie's non-sequitur seemed to take him by surprise.

"Soybeans. Mostly soybeans."

"What time did you plant in the summer?"

"We planted in the spring, ma'am. Usually in April."

Which I learned later was the correct answer despite Annie's attempt to mislead the boy.

Afterwards, back in his office, Sheriff Granger was still unconvinced.

"I don't know what that kid's game is, but he's still lying."

"Yes," Annie agreed, "some of the time, and he's being intentionally vague about a number of things, but I still think he's Ethan Miller."

"Well, I'll let you figure it out, Annie. I've got to catch the early train tomorrow to Newark."

He opened a drawer, pulled out an impressive looking silver badge, and handed it to Annie. I wondered if there'd be some kind of swearing-in ceremony, but there was nothing of the kind. Annie took the badge and slipped it in one of her pockets.

"Be careful, Annie," he said. Then he looked at me. "You too, young lady."

"Yes, sir."

13. Letter to Mr. Frank Butler

Tuesday, March 13, 1900

Dearest,

I guess the terrible death of our friend Jane Dalton has affected me more than I'd care to admit. For some reason, which is surely related, I've been thinking a lot about the time we were in Europe, maybe ten years ago, and we read in the newspapers that I was dead.

Do you remember that one of the German papers had a picture of me shrouded in black mourning flags? Supposedly, I'd died in Buenos Aires of pneumonia. It was very disconcerting. Being alive, yet thought to be dead.

We were, of course, most concerned about my dear mother, whom we later discovered had cried for two days until she learned the truth. You, of course, as always, took care of everything, alerting newspapers everywhere that I was fine, and if I remember correctly, "enjoying splendid health."

Death certainly leaves a trail behind it, and that

experience, of course, compelled me to think about it quite a bit. Now our dear friend has suddenly died, and I'm sure that everyone in the town, like me, is having death-related musings. I've already spoken to young Miss Lizzie about it, and she seems to be doing all right. I'm trying to keep her focused on the resolution (hopefully) of our various mysteries.

As for the young boy, he's now admitted that he's Ethan Miller, Lizzie's brother. The sheriff still isn't convinced, thinking that the boy is faking a false identity to take advantage of the sympathy it generates. But I'm convinced. Entirely. Actually, I was convinced from the first moment I saw him. The first time I spoke with Ethan in his cell, he shrugged. Just like Lizzie does. You know that little shrug? I'm sure you do. You notice everything. But far more substantial evidence has come to light, including a distinguishing burn on his left forearm, that seems to me, what do the lawyers say? dispositive.

Something else quite curious has come to light. Lizzie and I have been going through the new documents that Jane had recently received from the library in Newark, and it seems that Judge Fairfax was the executor of Rebecca Miller's will and testament, which has apparently been kept a secret all these years. Why? Am I wrong to be suspicious that the judge might be Lizzie's father? Have I become too distrustful of everything and everyone? Later tonight, at my evening prayers, I'll ask God to forgive my presumptive and

slanderous thoughts, and I'll pray for the truth.
Then I'll pray for you, my love.
Your loving Missie

14. Annie Oakley

Wednesday, March 14, 1900

How does one describe a woman . . .

Who's a friend of William McKinley, Jr., the current president of the United States, who once honored Miss Annie, his fellow native Ohioan, at the Columbian Exposition in Chicago when he was the Governor of Ohio.

Who knows and is much admired by Queen Victoria, Mr. Gladstone, Kaiser Wilhelm II, King Umberto of Italy, President Carno of France, etc.

Who's friends with Buffalo Bill, Mr. Thomas Edison, Sitting Bull, Mark Twain, etc.

Who starred in the play, *Deadwood Dick*, getting enthusiastic reviews, until the show's manager, John Keenan, absconded with the receipts.

Who can split a card held edgewise at ninety feet (which I know sounds impossible, but I've seen her do it many times, and so has everyone else who's ever attended a Wild West Show).

Who shoots the corks off bottles, the flames off candles spinning on a wheel, and dimes tossed into the air at ninety feet.

Who once shot the ashes off the cigarette of Kaiser Wilhelm II.

Who once shot a hundred tossed targets in succession, a feat never accomplished by a woman and only achieved by a handful of men.

Who can hit every target while standing on a moving horse.

Who can run a hundred yards in thirteen seconds, is an accomplished fencer, and a master of the lariat.

Who's my dear friend and mentor.

Much like a mother.

When I determined to record this account of the present events and mysteries in Nutley, New Jersey, I assumed that there'd be no reason to document the well-known facts about Annie Oakley's life. After all, she's famous all over the world, and everyone knows her story. It seemed as superfluous as recounting the facts of the life of Mrs. Ida McKinley!

Then I met Ethan, and I realized that there are some people in this world who would need to know more. When I mentioned my dilemma to my father he said:

"Well, how much do you *really* know about Queen Victoria, my dear?"

Not very much.

So I've decided to include the subsequent (very brief) recapitulation of the facts of Miss Annie's life. Those of you who are fully familiar with her history can readily skip the next few paragraphs.

Annie's parents were Quakers from Pennsylvania who moved to the far western frontier of Ohio, where they rented a farm and raised their seven surviving children. Phoebe Anne Mosey, known as Annie, was born in the family's small log cabin on August 13th, 1860. When she was five years old, her father was caught in a blizzard and eventually died of the repercussions. Specifically, a deadly pneumonia. Annie's mother, Susan, unable to support the entire family, sent Annie and one of her sisters to the Darke County Infirmary for orphans, indigents, and legally classified "idiots."

Later in that same year, Annie was "bound out" to a horrible couple as a family servant. With the exception, I'm sure, of Mr. Frank, Annie has never discussed her two years as a virtual and much-abused slave. When she was eleven years old, she ran away, eventually returning to her mother's home.

When Annie was eight years old, to help feed the family, she shot a squirrel with an old cap-and-ball Kentucky rifle. In time, the family began shipping Annie's game to exclusive restaurants in Cincinnati, and by the time she was fifteen, she'd paid off her mother's mortgage.

Then she met Frank.

Is the legend true?

Yes, it's true.

Frank Butler, an Irish immigrant, was a renowned American sharpshooter who made his living by giving marksman exhibitions around the country, often taking side bets to compete against local marksmen. On Thanksgiving Day, 1875, Butler was in Cincinnati for a shooting performance, and he agreed to a challenge offered by Jack Frost, who owned a local hotel. The bet was for $100, and Frank had no idea who his opponent would be.

His opponent, of course, was a tiny fifteen-year-old county girl, barely five feet tall, with a rifle almost as big as she was. But Frank was gracious, ever the gentleman, and the competition began. Annie hit every one of her twenty-five targets, but Frank missed on his very last shot.

The unknown little country girl had beaten the famous marksman, but Frank took it right in stride, having nothing but admiration and respect for his victor.

They were married a year later.

When Annie was sixteen years old.

One year older than me.

To this day, they still seem like loving newlyweds.

The rest of it you probably know:

Frank took over the business and promotion, and they eventually joined with Colonel Cody and his Wild West Show. Annie quickly became the main attraction, second-billed after the Colonel himself, and the highest paid.

One of the highest-paid women in the country, in fact.

Maybe the highest.

Annie and Frank traveled all around the country and all around the world with the Colonel, who always maintained his primary campgrounds in the New York City area. Eventually, the Butlers fell in love with Nutley, New Jersey, and built their house right next door to Dr. Carlyle in 1893.

Sometimes it's called "Oakley House."

So how does one describe a woman who is kind, generous, humble, and compassionate? So ladylike?

(Also pretty.)

With a sense of humor.

The Quakers talk about the "divine within," something they call the "inner light," which always seems aglow from within my dear Miss Annie.

Maybe you're wondering about her flaws?

No one's perfect. Right?

Well, I've known Miss Annie for six years, and this is the best I can do:

She has absolutely no truck with laziness, malingering, or tardiness. She can sometimes be a bit punctilious about things, a bit of a stickler. Although a world-famous performer and very independent woman, she's also surprisingly shy.

(Sorry if you were hoping for more than that.)

Miss Annie goes through life with a marked confidence, devoid of ego. She never discusses her own accomplishments, and she's always far more interested in others than in herself.

She once gave me the best advice I've ever received:

"Girls should occupy their minds with other people's troubles."

Which I try to do each and every day.

15. The Lady, or the Tiger?

Wednesday, March 14, 1900

I spent the morning at the orphanage, just like every other Wednesday, teaching a reading class and catching up with old friends. After a few rounds of hopscotch and jump rope with the girls, we settled down in the little classroom and read out loud *The Lady, or the Tiger?*

The children were especially excited about the story, since the author, Frank R. Stockton, once lived right here in Nutley. He was originally from Philadelphia, actually descended from Richard Stockton who'd signed the *Declaration of Independence*, and he moved to Nutley, into a house on Walnut Street, after his marriage to Marian Tuttle. Originally, he'd been an engraver, but in time he became a famous writer, poet, and editor.

In 1867, Stockton and his wife left town and returned to Philadelphia. He was suffering from serious and chronic problems with his eyesight, and he'd always been lame as well. From what I've been told by his Nutley friends and acquaintances, he was a good-humored man who was very well-liked.

As far as I know, he's still living and writing in Pennsylvania.

I suppose he's most famous for his clever fairy tales, but everyone knows his short story about the young man in some ancient country who's condemned to stand alone in a crowded amphitheater and choose between the door on the left or the door on the right.

Contemplating "incorruptible chance":

Since behind one of the doors is a beautiful woman who will marry him immediately, and behind the other door is a ravenous tiger who will tear him to bits.

Of course, the reason that he's in this terrible predicament is that he fell in love with the King's daughter, who also fell in love with him. As the princess sits in the amphitheater watching, she knows two important things.

She knows *who* the beautiful woman is. A woman she absolutely detests and considers a romantic rival.

She also knows which door the woman is standing behind.

Well, you all know the end of the story, but my kids didn't, and they were absolutely stunned when the author refused to reveal what happened.

The young man looks up, into the audience, sees the princess, and she indicates the door on the right.

Which he chooses.

But when the door opens, is it the lady or the tiger? Stockton refuses to tell us.

I leave it with all of you.

It's hard to think of anything more unsatisfying, more of a trick or a gimmick, but there's no denying that it's unforgettable.

It also compels us to do what Stockton tells us to do. Decide for ourselves. Eventually, when the children recuperated from their crushing disappointment, they started to wonder what the princess had done. And why? Had she given up her lover to her hated rival? Or had she, in jealousy, given him to the tiger.

She was, as Stockton makes clear, "hot-blooded," "imperious," "semi-barbaric," and suffering from "the combined fires of despair and jealousy."

I once read somewhere that the story is about a dilemma that's "unsolvable," but I think it's more about whether the young man (meaning all of us) can trust the one he loves.

After allowing the kids to kick it around for a while, I offered no definitive answer. Then I walked back home, convinced that the tiger emerged from the door on the right.

Believing that jealousy is a *very* powerful motive.

16. Will and Testament

Wednesday, March 14, 1900

To whom does a spinster leave what little she has?

Despite the pervasive sorrow lingering in the town after Miss Dalton's tragic death, there was also considerable, yet mostly unspoken, curiosity about the deposition of her will. Miss Jane always dressed rather nicely, and she was never, in any way, destitute, but some of her friends did wonder how she'd managed to survive on the pittance she received from the town to run our makeshift library and oversee our legal records and documents.

Despite this widespread curiosity, there were only four of us in the small conference room at Franklin Trust: Judge Fairfax; Mayor Langley, who was also the director of the bank; Miss Annie, representing Sheriff Granger; and me, as Annie's tag-a-long.

The judge sat at the end of the table with the will lying in front of him. He was probably in his early sixties, wearing a handsome dark suit, with impressive gray-white hair and still-handsome features. I'd always liked the man. He was well respected by everyone, with a reputation for fair-mindedness and generosity. But all I could think about was the fact that he knew my dead mother and that he'd never mentioned the fact.

Not once.

Which seemed very peculiar, if not suspicious.

"I hope," the mayor suggested, "you'll summarize things, Owen."

"That'll be fine, Warren," the judge agreed. "Then, if any of you wish, you can read the document in its entirety."

We waited.

"The truth is," he continued, "Miss Dalton leaves an estate valued at approximately $94,558, being the compilation of $90,346 currently in her bank account right here at Franklin Trust and $4,212, the estimated value of her home on Mulberry Street. She leaves a sum of $20,000 to St. Mary's Orphanage, and the remainder, $74,558, to Mrs. Frances Langley."

We were stunned.

All of us.

Both by the amount and by her primary heir. Where did Miss Jane possibly get over $90,000 in cash? And why Miss Fanny? They were good friends, it's true, and everyone liked Fanny Langley, but Miss Jane had numerous friends, many of whom would have been able to benefit far more from such an inheritance than the wife of the mayor.

Almost in unison, Annie and I looked over at the mayor. He seemed even more astonished than the rest of us.

"Are you certain, Owen?" he asked.

"I am, Warren. It's sitting right here in front of me."

During the past two days, I'd discovered that death creates all kinds of strange silences, and this one, the reading-of-the-will silence, was especially odd.

"Is the figure correct?" the judge wondered.

"I have no idea," the mayor admitted, "but I can check it easily enough."

He stood up to leave.

"Maybe," the judge suggested, "you could ask Fanny to stop by."

The mayor and his wife lived right down the street. Three houses away, in fact.

"Of course, I'll send someone to get her."

Completely baffled, he exited the room.

Annie looked at Judge Fairfax.

"Did you draw up the will, Owen?"

"I did, Annie," he explained. "About three months ago. The amount of cash is based on her most recent bank statement."

"Do you have any idea where her money came from?"

"No, she never told me, but whenever I see surprising amounts like this, especially from people with negligible incomes, it's usually a matter of an earlier inheritance. Jane's only sister died a number of years ago in New York, so maybe that had something to do with it. But I'm surprised that Warren is surprised."

He smiled.

"I thought Warren knew everything about everyone's finances."

Annie nodded.

Then she did what I was hoping she would do.

"You've done many wills over the years, haven't you, Owen?"

"I have."

He made no reference to my mother.

"Were you doing them back in 1887? Thirteen years ago?"

"Yes, that was back before the judgeship came along."

But that was it.

Even with Annie baiting him, even with me sitting right across the table, he never mentioned my mother. It seemed to me, although maybe I was seeing what wasn't really there, that the judge was rather uneasy, something that was very rare for a man of such marked equanimity.

He stood up.

"I'll check on Warren."

Which we knew was unnecessary.

It was the first time that I'd ever seen someone eager to leave a room with Annie Oakley in it.

When the judge was gone, I looked at Miss Annie.

"Why won't he mention my mother?"

"I don't know."

"But you have your speculations."

Annie laughed her soft and lovely laugh. I was always happy when I could make her laugh.

"Yes, my dear, I'm sure that Mr. Frank would verify that I have far too many of those."

I smiled, but I didn't let her off the hook.

"Then tell me."

She wondered if she should, then she decided that she probably should.

"I wonder if there was a relationship of some kind. An attraction of some kind."

I'd wondered too.

"Do you think he's the 'someone' who puts flowers on my mother's grave every year?"

"I don't know, Lizzie."

I took it a step further.

"Is he the mysterious figure who fired over my head in the graveyard?"

"I'd certainly like to think that he wasn't."

Then I got to the uncomfortable part.

"Do you mean *romantic* attraction?"

"I don't know what I mean, my dear, but whatever it was, he certainly seems disinterested in discussing it. But let's be very careful and not let our imaginations get the best of us."

It was hard not to.

My mother was a pretty young widow back then, which was around the same time that Veronica Fairfax went through her reputed "change" after the miscarriage of her third child. Had their marriage gone cold? Had there been an attraction between the lawyer and the widow? Had it led to anything? It was almost impossible for me to fathom, given everything that I'd ever heard about my mother's reputation. Not to mention the judge's stellar reputation for integrity and propriety.

"Let's not get ahead of ourselves, Lizzie," Annie warned, as if reading my thoughts.

I agreed, nodding my agreement.

She put her hand gently on my right shoulder, as a mother might do, as if to say "everything will be all right, my dear."

I certainly hoped that she was right.

Eventually, the judge and the mayor returned with a completely flustered Fanny.

She looked down at Annie.

"How can this be?" she wondered. "Why me?"

Annie, as always, was compassionate.

"It's what Jane wanted, Fanny. You were *always* close friends. Maybe the question is really, 'Why not you?'"

It seemed to help.

Fanny looked at her husband.

"Where did she get all that money?"

"I have no idea. I just looked through her records

and most of it was deposited in a single transaction over a decade ago, before I was appointed director of the bank."

"In the end," the judge pointed out, "it really doesn't matter. Jane wanted you to have the money, Fanny, and I'll be glad to make the arrangements."

Fanny was still flustered.

"What will everyone think?"

It was directed at Annie.

"I think that everyone will think that a kind and thoughtful friend left her estate to one of her closest friends."

This seemed to calm Fanny down. She could accept this strange turn of events if no one would think it untoward or somehow inappropriate.

"I need to get myself to the courthouse in Belleview," the judge announced rather abruptly, before rising, nodding to the ladies, then leaving the room.

Finally, Fanny sat down at the table with her husband beside her.

$74,558 was slowly sinking in.

"Could I ask a rather impolite question," Annie asked, which seemed rather odd since Annie was *always* polite.

"Of course," the mayor responded, assuming the question related to the money.

"You were seen on the bridge with Miss Jane the day before she died."

It wasn't actually a question.

But it was.

The mayor didn't seem to mind. He was fully aware that the sheriff had asked Annie to "look into" Miss Jane's supposedly accidental death.

"Yes, Annie. It's no secret that I disagreed with Jane about the disposition of the newly arrived documents from Newark. *All* of our legal documents in fact. Jane believed that they should be open to the public, but I believed, and still believe, that people's personal and legal records should be held in trust by the town and available only to those related to the documents. Excepting, of course, police and judicial matters."

"You argued about it?"

"We did. As much as anyone could argue with Jane. But I must admit I was rather surprised by what seemed to me her reversal of attitude. Jane Dalton knew more about everyone in this town – and all our secrets – than anyone. Including me. And she'd always employed the utmost discretion. She was, in fact, the keeper of the town's secrets. But opening the new files to public scrutiny might expose secrets that had no right being exposed."

"Are you thinking about anything in particular, Warren?"

"I'm not. But everyone has secrets, Annie, and I think they should be respected."

"I do as well. Unless, as you say, they relate to matters of the law or law enforcement."

"Exactly."

Even though there seemed to be a consensus in the room, I couldn't help wondering if it was the Mayor's own secrets that he was so eager to protect.

Then he felt as though he needed to say something more.

In his own defense.

"Like everyone else in this town, I loved our dear Miss Jane, and now that she's gifted this astonishing kindness to my wife, I feel terrible that I ever argued with her at all."

Fanny summarized her own thoughts much more simply.

"She was an angel."

No one disagreed.

17. Circus

Wednesday, March 14, 1900

A young woman stood perilously, it seemed to me, on a high wire.

She looked down at Annie and waved.

Standing next to Annie, my heart was galloping within my chest, and I felt a bit nauseous. I've never been enthusiastic about heights. What did Dr. Johnson say? That heights are very beautiful, but they should be observed from down below. Something like that. At the present moment, even though I was watching the high-wire girl from down below, my heart was agitated, panicked, accelerated.

She waved again.

Without a net.

"Her name's Sabrina," Annie pointed out.

Well, I wish Sabrina would stop waving and start concentrating on getting herself to the other side of the arena. Which she finally did, slowly, gradually, as my poor heart banged around within my chest with each and every death-defying step forward, even though she was moving as casually as if she were walking down the riverbank.

Annie and I were standing in the circus arena of Eaton Stone's headquarters on Kingsland Avenue. I know it probably seems odd, but Eaton Stone, the famous circus man and legendary daredevil equestrian, lived right here in Nutley. He was the first man to do a somersault on a moving bareback horse, along with a number of other hard-to-believe stunts. Eventually, he settled down in Nutley, building a number of professional training arenas for a wide range of circus performers: acrobats, marksmen, trapeze and high-wire performers, bareback riders, and a few clowns. It was on a trip to visit Mr. Stone in 1892 that Annie had fallen in love with the little town of Nutley and determined to live here.

Two years later, in 1894, during Annie's first full year in Nutley, she and Henry Bunner, the distinguished editor of *Puck Magazine*, who also lived in Nutley, decided to organize an "amateur" circus to benefit the American Red Cross.

I was nine years old at the time, and Sr. Agnes and the other good sisters took all of their orphans to see the circus, which certainly didn't seem "amateur" to us.

There were fencing exhibitions, trained dogs, high wire acts, trapeze performers, countless clowns, pink cotton candy, popcorn, even a huge dancing bear. With, of course, Annie Oakley as the main attraction, performing numerous amazing feats, such as shooting targets a hundred feet behind her with a mirror and shooting targets while standing on top of a moving horse.

It was the highlight of my youth, and everyone in town agreed that it was one of the most memorable days in the history of Nutley, along with the 1880 visit of President Ulysses S. Grant.

Then I realized that I was all alone.

Annie had wandered off to talk to one of Mr. Stone's stable boys, making arrangements for our trip tomorrow morning.

Which I was excited about.

Earlier, we'd gone to the Nutley Supply Store after the reading of Miss Dalton's will at the bank. Annie wanted to talk to some of the customers, especially the various farmers and salesmen who came to Nutley from out of town. Generally, people feel very comfortable talking to Annie, and the men today were no exception. Over and over, she described the farm that Ethan had told us about, with an emphasis on the few specifics that he'd mentioned within his vague recollections:

A twenty-acre soybean farm
A log cabin and a barn
A narrow river in the northwest corner
High gray mountains off to the west
With one much higher than the rest
And something called the "300 Steps"

Most of the men just shrugged, but eventually she found a farmer who'd heard of the 300 Steps.

"Where are they?" she wondered.

"Western New Jersey," he remembered, "near Hanover at Watnong Mountain."

Then he added:

"But I've never seen them myself, and some say they don't even exist."

Annie was unperturbed.

Afterwards, we met with Mrs. Fairfax in the manager's office. Veronica Fairfax still owned Nutley's only supply store, which had been founded by one of her ancestors over fifty years ago. But she didn't actually manage the store, and she was seldom there most days, but early this morning, Annie had sent her a message, so she was waiting patiently in the manager's office. As always, she was dressed in a finely-tailored dress, with lots of lovely lace, especially at the collar and the sleeves. She looked as exquisite and elegant as always.

After nodding politely at me and smiling, she turned to Annie.

"How can I help?"

"I'm wondering if you carry Porter & Ward flannels? Men's long sleeves?"

I'm sure a question about men's shirts wasn't what Mrs. Fairfax was expecting, but she did her best.

"I believe I know the shirts you're asking about,

Annie. They used to be quite popular with farmers and farmhands, but we've never carried them here at the store."

"Do you know who might? Anywhere in New Jersey?"

"Hanover Feed and Supply once carried Porter & Ward clothing. Maybe they still do."

"Anyone else?"

"I'm sure you could find them in the city. Maybe even in Newark. Would you like me to check?"

"No, that's all right, Veronica, you've already been a great help."

I had the distinct feeling that Mrs. Fairfax was dying of curiosity, but she never bothered to ask why Annie was so interested in Porter & Ward. Instead, she changed the subject.

"I heard about the disposition of the will this morning."

"Yes," Annie nodded, "I suppose it's a bit of a surprise."

Mrs. Fairfax seemed unsurprised.

"I'm glad for Fanny."

She seemed perfectly sincere, but she couldn't resist adding:

"I'm sure she can use the money."

Which surprised me.

Why would the wife of the mayor, who was also the director of the local bank, need money?

"Why is that, Veronica?" Annie asked.

Mrs. Fairfax was a woman of breeding, so she never shrugged. But if she ever made an exception, I had the feeling that she might do so right now.

"Things are much tighter than they seem," she answered rather cryptically.

Which, I could tell, surprised Miss Annie, who knew Fanny Langley at least as well as Mrs. Fairfax.

"Besides," the judge's wife said, almost off-handedly, "there's the matter of the mayor."

What?

What did *that* mean?

But Annie, to my consternation, left it right there, and Mrs. Fairfax looked at me and changed the subject.

"Do you think that young boy is your brother, dear?"

"I do."

"Well then, despite whatever's happened before, I'm very glad for the both of you."

Again, she was perfectly sincere.

"Thank you. I must admit, it's both strange and exciting."

She understood, then she looked back at Annie.

"I understand that he's been released, and that he's staying with the deputy. At least, temporarily."

"I didn't know that," Annie admitted, "but I'm glad you've told me. It's very kind of Lawrence to take him in."

"Very kind, indeed," Mrs. Fairfax agreed.

Later, after we'd taken our leave, when we were

out on the street heading home, I couldn't contain myself.

"What did she mean by 'the matter of the mayor'?"

Annie stopped in the street, turned, and looked at me directly.

"Do you want me to treat you like an adult young woman?"

"Always."

She nodded.

"There have always been rumors about the mayor," she explained. "I have no idea if they're true."

"I understand."

Nothing more was said about it, but I was old enough to know what "rumors" meant.

That the mayor had a mistress.

Or mistresses.

18. Valentine

Wednesday, March 14, 1900

Did I mention I like to dance?

I also liked being asked to dance!

The wooden dance floor at the Old Military Hall was crowded with dancers tonight as a versatile local band – fiddle, banjo, and mandolin – played a lively and lovely variety of waltzes, two-steps, and even quadrilles.

The theme was Valentine's Day, and the hall was beautifully decorated with flickering Japanese lanterns and red-and-pink paper hearts. Last month, a terrible snow-and-ice storm had cancelled our annual Valentine's Day Dance, and the township committee wisely postponed the dance for a month. So this year, our popular Valentine's Day Dance was on March 14th, not February 14th, and no one seemed to mind.

I was wearing a white cotton dress that I'd sewn under Annie's meticulous guidance, with modified mutton sleeves, lace everywhere she permitted it, and the skirt drawn neatly at the waist. It was (I'm certain it's vain to say) a bit of a sensation, although I probably should admit that the dress got more compliments than I did!

So, I danced with my best friend Jimmy Granger, who looked as sharp and handsome as could be, with his dark hair actually combed, wearing a new black suit that I'd never seen before, along with his perpetually alluring smile.

I also danced, of course, with Mr. Palmer, ever-elegant in an expensive-looking light-gray dress coat, perfectly tailored dress pants, and fashionable high-collared shirt.

I also danced with my ever-attentive deputy, Lawrence Langley, who'd arrived in a brand-new uniform, dark blue with tasteful gold trim, looking quite the dashing figure.

I also danced with lots of other men too, both young and older, who seemed to line up patiently and wait their turns.

After a particularly wonderful waltz with Lawrence, the band announced a well-deserved break, and Annie came over after dancing with the mayor.

"Doesn't Lawrence look quite the figure in his bright new uniform?" Annie said to Lawrence's proud father.

"Should a father compliment his son?" the mayor kidded.

"Of course," Annie said. "Especially tonight."

"I'm very proud," the mayor admitted proudly.

He patted his son gently on the shoulder, bowed to both Annie and me, then vanished back into the crowd, obviously looking for his wife Fanny.

"It's good to see him pleased," Lawrence admitted. "I wasn't always a source of pride."

Miss Annie seemed as surprised as I was.

"What do you mean, Lawrence?" I wondered out loud.

Maybe I shouldn't have asked, but I wasn't able to contain my curiosity.

"Oh, I was a bit of a fool when I was younger, Lizzie. A bit wild. But all that's in the distant past. Thank goodness."

It was quite an admission, and despite my curiosity, I felt it improper to press him any further, but Annie had a quite different question.

"Was that here in Nutley, Lawrence? Or in Manasquan?"

"It was here, Miss Annie, before you moved to town. I've spent most of my life right here in Nutley."

"I thought you were born in Manasquan?"

"I was, but we left when I was still a child."

Which both Annie and I knew wasn't true.

Was it a lie?

Or was it possible that Lawrence didn't know where he was born?

Then Theresa Morning Dove walked by with Mrs. Fairfax, and I gave her a little wave.

She smiled and nodded right back.

But Lawrence was pensive.

Finally, he turned to Annie.

"I never told you this before, but I saw Mr. Palmer with Miss Theresa last week. They were talking at the edge of the woods near the river. I didn't know what to make of it."

"What were they doing?"

"Talking."

"Did it seem pre-arranged?"

"I have no idea. When they saw me in the distance, Theresa waved, Palmer nodded politely, and they immediately parted in different directions."

"Why didn't you mention this before?"

"It seemed like nothing."

"Then why mention it now?"

"I don't know," he admitted. "I guess I've become suspicious of everyone, Miss Annie. You've got me convinced that someone pushed Miss Jane off Centre Bridge."

Such thoughts of dear Miss Jane were very sobering and intrusive in the midst of our "Valentine's Day" fun and frivolity. But such serious thoughts were soon banished by the lively appearance of Miss Fanny, who, it was clear, had fully acquiesced to her unanticipated inheritance and was now back to being her typical jolly and congenial self.

Then I spotted what I was looking for across the crowded dance floor.

My brother.

He looked totally out of place, wearing ill-fitting clothes obviously borrowed from Lawrence Langley, and wishing that he was anywhere else in the world.

Since I couldn't take a chance that he might disappear, I said "Excuse me" to Annie and the others, then started for the other side of the hall.

Sure enough, I saw him heading for the hall's back exit, but I caught him at the door.

"Ethan."

He turned around and seemed pleased to see me.

"I'm so glad you came," I said.

"Well, I only came because Lawrence said you wanted me to come."

I understood.

"Don't worry, Ethan, you'll get used to things. I'm sure it's difficult."

He shrugged the shrug that Annie had told me looked exactly like my own shrug, which she also told me wasn't exactly ladylike, so I've been doing my best to control my unfortunate habit.

But I must admit, it looked just fine on a young man like Ethan.

I continued, maybe a bit too excitedly.

"Guess what? You can come and live with me, Ethan! Dr. Carlyle telegrammed his invitation last night."

When Ethan didn't respond, I gave him even more good news.

"Miss Annie has also offered you a room, right next door to my own house, if you think you'd be more comfortable over there."

He looked into my eyes.

"I'm not comfortable anywhere."

I wanted to cry.

I wanted to sit right down in one of the chairs and cry, but I didn't.

Maybe he realized.

"I'm sorry to feel so sorry for myself, Elizabeth, but I'd be lying if I pretended that I'm not confused and overwhelmed."

"Which is exactly why you need to be with me," I assured him.

He nodded.

"You're right. Just give me a few more days with Lawrence. I feel rather comfortable at his small place, where I'm alone most of the time."

It was hard to imagine.

I'd grown up without brothers or sisters or a mother or a father, which, of course, made me feel very much alone in this world. But I always knew, deep in my heart, that I was never *really* alone. I had Sr. Agnes, and all the other good sisters, and all my young friends at the orphanage. So even for me, who'd spent most of her life as an orphan, it was impossible to imagine Ethan's life, entirely alone, living in an old barn, with bogus parents as his only human contact.

Oddly enough, Ethan nodded toward Theresa who

was standing near the stage talking with Annie and the mayor.

"Who's that?"

I wasn't sure whom he meant.

"The pretty one with the long dark hair."

"That's Theresa Morning Dove. She lives with Miss Annie."

"What kind of name is that?"

"She's a Lakota Indian from South Dakota."

It didn't help, and I realized.

"Do you know where South Dakota is?"

"No. I don't even know *what* it is."

He didn't seem particularly ashamed. It was just the truth of the matter.

He continued.

"To be honest, Elizabeth, I don't know *what* an Indian is. It seems that I don't know much of anything."

"But you can learn, Ethan."

"Yes, I suppose I can."

"Will you let me help you?"

"Yes, in time, but I'd like to go now. Things will take me some time."

"I understand."

He nodded again.

"It's wonderful to have my big brother back in my life."

He smiled, which was also wonderful. I'd never seen him smile before.

Then he turned, stopped, and looked across the

room at Theresa again.

"I saw her that day at the librarian's house."

I was astonished.

"When?"

"The day the sheriff arrested me."

"Before Miss Jane died? Or afterwards?"

"Before. She came to the house, went inside, and left a few minutes later."

"Was Miss Jane there?"

"No. I never saw her. Never."

Then he shrugged again, and he left.

I watched him go as the band started tuning up, but I didn't feel like dancing again. I needed a few moments all to myself, so I got my shawl and went out beneath the stars. It was cold outside, but a number of impervious young men were lurking about, some smoking, some, I'm certain, drinking from their pocket flasks. But when the music started again, they immediately went back inside, and I sat down on a small bench. All alone. The bench was bitter cold, and I knew I wouldn't last too long, but I needed a bit of solitude.

Not to think about the terrible death of poor Miss Jane, but to think about the terribly lonely life of my brother, Ethan, who'd now been thrust into a world that he had no comprehension of, nor knowledge of. He could probably use farming tools and implements effectively, but he seemed to have no idea about the world outside that isolated farm. The *real* world. I doubted if he knew who George Washington was. I doubted if he knew what Christmas was. I doubted if he knew what love was.

It was terrible, and it made the chilly March night even colder than it was, and I suddenly craved the company of my friends and neighbors inside, enjoying the music, enjoying the dancing, enjoying each other.

Even though one of them was a monster.

A murderer.

When I hear a slight noise from behind me, it startled me. Suddenly, a rough sack of some kind was forced over my head and the barrel of a rifle was pressed into the back of my neck.

It happened so fast that I had no chance to react, but my heart did, exploding into a wild disordered sprint.

"Stand up."

It was a man's voice.

Unrecognizable.

I did as I was told, and a hand immediately grabbed my right arm and led me away from the music. It was clear that there were at least two people guiding me towards the woods.

Maybe three.

I wanted to be brave, but I wasn't sure what I could possibly do. Running away seemed quite impossible. Fighting seemed equally foolish. So I prayed a bit.

We didn't go far.

"Stop."

Terrified, I did as I was told.

"What do you want?" I said, my voice oddly muffled under the harsh burlap hood.

"Leave well enough alone."

The voice was firm and threatening.

I said nothing.

Then the hood over my head began to tighten, as if there was a ligature around my neck, and I was simultaneously knocked to the ground. Instinctively, I struggled to relieve the pressure at my neck with both of my hands, and, eventually, I was able to remove the hood and stand up in the night.

They were gone.

Whoever they were.

For a moment, I stood alone in the darkness and looked up gratefully at the stars. Then I started for the music. My father was off in Newark helping people injured in a train crash, but Miss Annie was here, inside the Old Military Hall, and I needed, once again, to find myself in her comforting and protective presence.

I stumbled along, wondering if my heart would ever slow down.

The band was playing a pretty song.

One I've always loved.

"The Blue Danube."

19. Letter to Mr. Frank Butler

Wednesday, March 14, 1900

My dearest,

Lizzie, of course, was the belle of the ball!

The beaus lined up to dance with our darling, but she seems to be keeping her senses about her. Quite naturally, she was in high yet still dignified spirits at the Valentine's Day Dance, although rather pensive in the aftermath during the ride home. Maybe she was worn out from all the attention.

She wore her lovely white dress, and I wore the red one you like so much, dancing with the mayor and the judge and many others, all the time wishing I was dancing with my handsome Frank Butler.

Ethan was also there briefly, acting oddly, distracted, and clearly out of place, but Lizzie did her best to comfort the young boy before he left. For the time being, he's staying at Lawrence's little cottage, but he knows that he's welcome both here and next door. Everything, I'm sure, will take time, and Lizzie seems fully aware of the fact.

I'm now convinced that Ethan was taken to western New Jersey after he was abducted/kidnapped twelve years ago.

I'm making various inquiries.

Don't worry!

Your loving Missie

20. Morristown

Thursday, March 15, 1900

We took the train to Morristown, secured our horses from the livestock car, and headed north toward Hanover.

There was a leather scabbard at Annie's saddle, and I knew the rifle from the stock:

> *Marlin Firearms Co., .22 caliber, Model 1891, lever action, side-loading, octagon 24" barrel, full-length mag tube, 2/3rd tubular magazine, fine bore, elite action, walnut stock.*

Annie was prepared.

Earlier, we sat together on the train, and I told her the truth.

"They put a hood over my head."

She was horrified yet somehow stoic at the same time.

"They?"

"Yes, only one of them spoke," I explained. "A man."

"Anything distinctive?"

"Nothing, I never recognized his voice. They led me into the woods, and he said, 'Leave well enough alone.'"

She thought it over.

"What," I wondered out loud, "are we supposed to leave alone? The death of Miss Jane? The truth about Ethan?"

"I'm not sure, Lizzie," she admitted. "Then what happened?"

"I struggled to remove the burlap bag, stood up, and they were gone."

She nodded, looking at me directly.

"I don't want you out of my sight."

I nodded.

It was fine with me.

Then Annie noticed the conductor standing at the front of the passenger car. It was now midday, the rush of the early morning travelers had passed, and the train was sparsely occupied.

"I'll be back."

She rose from her seat and made her way to the conductor, a pleasant-looking man in his mid-fifties. They spoke casually, and I wondered if the man recognized who she was. Most probably. When Annie was dressed in normal women's apparel, she looked like any other pretty little woman in her late thirties. But today we were riding, and Annie was wearing her riding clothes, which, of course, she'd both designed and sewn:

> *A knee-length skirt of tan gabardine with fringe at the hem, a loose cotton tan blouse buttoned up the front to the collar, pearl-buttoned leggings, a dark broad-brimmed hat known these days (because of Annie) as a "cowgirl's hat," with her dark hair hanging loose and flowing down her back.*

In other words, she looked like Annie Oakley.

Since I couldn't hear what they were saying, I looked out the window and watched the beautiful world pass by, the beautiful New Jersey countryside, with fields, and forests, and distant hovering mountains.

I love trains.

I suppose everyone does, gliding along with such raw power and easy comfort, tunneling through the wide beautiful world outside one's window.

Annie was back, taking her seat beside me.

I didn't bother to ask her what she was up to, I just gave her my "asking" look.

"He's from the Morristown area," Annie explained, "so I asked him about the 300 Steps."

Ah, the mystery of the 300 Steps!

I waited.

"The 300 Steps," Annie smiled, "are three hundred granite steps built into the side of Watnong Mountain near Hanover. They climb the southface, zigzagging towards the summit."

"With what purpose?"

"Well, there are quite a few theories according to the conductor."

"I certainly hope you're going to tell me!"

Which she did.

"The most mundane, I suppose, is that they were built by miners working at a place called Malley's Quarry."

"I hope you can do better than that!"

She smiled.

"Another possibility is that they were built, maybe hundreds of years ago, by the Lenni-Lenape tribe. Maybe for mountain rituals."

Which was certainly intriguing.

"Another possibility," Annie continued, "is that the steps were built by Washington's troops when he was encamped at Morristown during the winter of 1777, or, maybe later, during the brutal winter of 1780."

"For what purpose?"

"Maybe as a lookout," Annie explained, "to keep an eye on British troop movements. It's a thousand-foot summit, and, apparently, it provides a wide and commanding view of the surrounding area. The conductor told me that General Washington often had his men set bonfires on the tops of local mountains to alert the patriots in the area of approaching Redcoats."

It was very inspiring, especially since later today we'd be riding through Washington country.

"But just like the farmer at the Nutley Supply Store," Annie added, "the conductor said that he'd never actually seen the 300 Steps, and that many people in the area believe they're a myth."

"Not me," I decided, fully aware that we'd never solve *that* mystery.

But we had much more important and pressing mysteries to try and unravel.

I looked out my window again, into the world outside, eager for adventure.

21. Hanover

Thursday, March 15, 1900

Kerosene was in the air.

Riding the narrow dirt roadway, we could see the flames rising above the treetops. When we reached the clearing, Annie pulled up Gypsy, and I did the same with Adler. Dismounting, we watched as the flames engulfed the barn.

I felt certain that it was the same barn where my brother had been imprisoned for twelve years. Now it was imploding in flames before our eyes, destroying any potential evidence.

The fire itself, I would have to admit, was rather mesmerizing, rather beautiful. I'd never seen such a tremendous fire before, reaching high into the afternoon sky. I could actually taste the burn in my mouth and feel the insidious heat pressing against my face. The predatory flames created a constant hum, as both the old wood of the barn and its reddish old paint cracked and popped and sizzled.

We'd had little trouble finding the place after our earlier visit to the Hanover Supply and Feed. The young clerk, dressed in his starched white shirt and bow tie, was more than willing to talk to Miss Annie Oakley.

About anything.

Yes, they sold Porter & Ward flannel shirts for men.

Yes, they sold Sellier & Bellot shotgun cartridges.

"Did any of your customers purchase both?" Annie wondered.

Maybe he shouldn't have, but the young clerk didn't seem to mind checking. He was more than eager to help, and Annie never even bothered to show her deputy badge.

We stood there, patiently, at the counter as the young man thumbed through several of the store's accounts books.

Then he looked back at Annie with a pleasant smile on his face.

"It looks like Mr. Randolph wears the shirts, and he sometimes uses Sellier & Bellot."

He clarified, "That's Mr. Jonas Randolph."

"I'd like to meet him," Annie said. "What's he like?"

"Very nice. Always congenial. He's a bit of an older man. I'd guess around sixty-five or so, and he and his missus have a farm about ten miles west."

"Any children?"

"No, but they usually hire a farm boy for planting

and harvest."

Annie asked for directions, thanked the young man, and we left the supply store.

I was surprised how easy it was.

Then we rode to the local sheriff's office in nearby Rockaway.

Which didn't go as well.

Earlier, I pointed out that most people instantly "take" to Annie, but there's always an occasional exception who gets his hackles up. Unfortunately, the local sheriff, Jason Bruckner, was one of those. I had the feeling that he wasn't comfortable about having a woman, and a tiny one at that, snooping around in his jurisdiction, supposedly on "police business," and asking questions about one of the local families.

Annie, of course, would have preferred his help, but I'm sure that she didn't expect the sheriff to drop whatever he was doing and ride out to the Randolph farm with two women he'd never met before. On the other hand, she didn't want to show up in his part of the county without letting him know what she was up to.

I guess it was more of a "courtesy call" than anything else, but it didn't go too well.

"Why do you want to talk with Jonas?"

"We have reason to believe he was involved in an abduction."

Annie's use of the pronoun "we," meant Sheriff Granger, of course. Not me.

"That's preposterous, ma'am. Abduction of

whom?"

"A young boy."

The sheriff registered his skepticism with something that was close to a sneer. Personally, I find sneers rather repulsive, and if I ever *did* sneer, which I've never done, and never would, I save my sneer for all the sneerers of the world.

"They don't have a boy."

"I'm told they have a farmhand."

"Yeah, a seasonal kid from the city. I bet he's out there right now, helping Jonas prep for planting."

"What's his name?"

"I don't know."

"William?" she suggested.

He shrugged. He didn't seem to know.

Then something occurred to him.

"When did this supposed abduction take place?"

"Twelve years ago."

He laughed.

"No offense, ma'am, but that's quite a tale. Jonas is a well-respected neighbor around here."

"I understand," Annie assured him. "I just want to talk to the man and his wife."

The sheriff shrugged a second time.

"Well, don't go making any unfounded accusations."

"I assure you, I'll be very pleasant, just as I've been with you."

Which must have made Bruckner realize that

maybe he hadn't been very pleasant himself.

"You ladies have a nice day."

He tipped his hat, and I gave him some credit for trying.

A loud explosion blasted from within the conflagration. Maybe an old paint can or something like that had ignited. It snapped me out of my reverie, and I noticed that Annie had pulled her Marlin.

"I'd like you to go back to Hanover, Lizzie, and wait for me there."

She was worried, but it was too late. A huge man, dressed in denim and old flannels, entered the clearing. He was well over six feet tall, powerful looking, with a dark full beard. Maybe in his mid-forties.

He clearly wasn't Jonas Randolph.

He was also holding a Remington 12-guage.

He came closer, then stopped at about fifty feet.

"You need to leave, little lady," he said to Annie. "This is private property."

He was threatening, intimidating, but he was also oddly polite.

Annie held her ground.

"Are you the arsonist?" she asked rather boldly.

Before he had a chance to answer, two other men, probably the man's brothers also appeared in the clearing, slowly approaching with their own shotguns. I'd seen both of them earlier at the feed store. They looked alike, maybe they were even twins, but not quite identical. With scruffy beards, but leaner and smaller than the big man, but also dressed in farmer denims. They also seemed to be aching for a fight, and I wished that I had my Winchester 32-20. I felt rather naked standing next to Annie with nothing to protect myself.

With no way to help her out.

The big man made an attempt to calm things down.

"It's not your concern, ma'am. It's my barn and my kerosene."

"You're lying," Annie assured him. "That barn belongs to Jonas Randolph.

The twins were fed up.

One of them, or maybe both of them, said:

"Beat it, lady!"

Then one of them made the mistake of raising his shotgun. I suspect that he was planning to shoot over our heads to scare us off.

Instantly, three shots rang out from right beside me.

The twin's rising shotgun was struck hard in the stock, close to the man's face, and the impact knocked it from his hands into the dirt.

At the same instant, the other twin's straw hat flew off his head into the flames, instantly devoured by the fire.

Also simultaneously, the button on the big man's shirt sleeve exploded, right next to his trigger hand, and the sleeve flapped open.

I didn't see any blood anywhere, but both the rapidity and the accuracy of Annie's three shots left the men clearly terrified.

Me, too!

For the last three years, Annie had been teaching me to shoot, and she'd taken me hunting over a dozen times. I would have to admit that I've become a pretty decent shot and that I know my way around firearms. I'd also seen several of her amazing performances and numerous practices. But this was *real* world, and these men were clearly dangerous, but now they were frightened of little Miss Annie.

Who was calm as calm could be.

"Put your guns on the ground."

It was amazing. It was like a dime novel about Wild Bill Hickok.

The men didn't hesitate. They did exactly as they were told.

Annie looked at the big man, the polite one.

"I may be a little lady, sir, but I've been authorized by Sheriff Richard Granger to speak to the Randolphs, and that's exactly what I intend to do."

"Jonas is our brother-in-law," he tried to explain. "He asked me to burn down his barn."

Annie didn't seem surprised.

"Where's the cabin?"

"Up the roadway to the left. Not far."

She seemed satisfied.

"You and your brothers can leave. You can come back later for your shotguns."

There was no argument.

The big man retreated immediately, and both he and his brothers vanished behind the smoldering barn.

Annie turned to me, still standing beside her uselessly.

"Are you all right, my dear?"

"I am."

She was thinking, and I knew exactly *what* she was thinking. She was thinking about sending me back to town before she went to the Randolphs' house.

"Let me come," I said with false bravado. "The trouble's over and done."

I guess she also believed the trouble was over.

She nodded, holstered her Marlin '91 at Gypsy's saddle, and we mounted our horses again.

22. Randolph

Thursday, March 15, 1900

We were sitting inside the little log cabin.

Ethan, of course, had said that his "parents," his abductors, lived in a log cabin.

Mrs. Randolph had opened the door.

"Sheriff Richard Granger sent us to ask you a few questions."

"Of course," she decided. "Come inside."

She was polite and hospitable.

Annie introduced herself as "Mrs. Anne Butler," and the woman insisted on preparing fresh tea.

She was a pleasant-looking farm wife, probably in her late thirties, wearing a pretty blue gingham house dress. She had ample auburn hair, pinned on top, with alert brown eyes. Overall, she was quite attractive.

As we waited for her return, Annie stood up and looked around the living room, and I did the same from my seat on the couch. The place was old, nicely furnished, comfortable, even cozy, with a lovely stone fireplace. Annie stepped over to the mantel and looked closely at the framed pictures. There were no boys.

No trace of Ethan.

When tea arrived, Jonas Randolph came in from the field, appearing much less muddied than I would have anticipated. After another round of introductions, he sat down in his chair and did his best to answer Annie's questions.

Neither the husband nor the wife seemed to realize that Anne Butler was Annie Oakley. Or maybe they were doing their best not to let on.

Jonas Randolph was tall and wiry, a powerful man, with a surprising shock of bright white hair above his weather-beaten face. He was clearly much older than his wife, and they seemed oddly matched, yet they seemed perfectly comfortable with each other's company. Jonas looked exactly like what he was, a man who'd spent a full lifetime working hard on a small farm in every kind of weather, through every kind of difficulty.

He chose his words carefully, didn't say anything he didn't have to, and I liked him. He seemed like a nice older man, and I wondered if I was nothing but a fool to think otherwise.

Was this the man who'd kidnapped my brother?

Was this the man who'd shot my mother three times in the back?

"I'd like to ask you," Annie began, "about the disappearance of a young boy."

The husband and the wife seemed baffled.

"I wouldn't know anything about that," Jonas assured her.

Annie was surely anticipating an answer like that, but she'd asked the question nonetheless, because she was doing what she always did. She was "reading" them both. The husband and the wife.

I was trying to do the same.

"It happened twelve years ago," Annie continued.

"In Hanover?" Mrs. Randolph wondered.

"No, in Nutley, in Franklin Township."

"I've never heard about it before," she assured us.

"Did you know a woman named Rebecca Miller?"

The wife shook her head "no," then she looked over at her husband who also shook his head.

"No."

"Did you ever know a man named Owen Fairfax? Now known as Judge Fairfax?"

"Never heard of him," the husband assured us. "The truth is, we mostly keep to the farm."

The wife agreed.

"I'm afraid we're not much help."

Annie pressed forward.

"I understand you have some help on the farm?"

"Yes," answered the wife, "a farm boy comes for parts of the year. During planting, then again during harvest season. The boys come from Newark, and they save their pay to help out their families back in the city. We try, if possible, to bring back the best kids for three or four years running."

"Do you have a boy right now?"

"Yes, Stephen. Stephen Tyler."

"Could I see his papers?"

"Of course."

Mrs. Randolph rose from her chair and left the room to retrieve the documents.

While she was gone, Annie stood up again, and went over to the gun rack, and pointed at a worn Parker shotgun.

I knew it well.

> *Parker Brothers, Meriden, Connecticut, 12-guage, double-barrel, 1882, Damascus steel*

It might have been the gun that killed my mother.

"May I?" Annie asked the husband.

"Of course."

Annie took it from the rack and checked the chambers.

I'd learned enough about shotguns to know that it was the kind of weapon that could easily handle Sellier & Bellot shotgun shells.

Annie looked at Jonas.

"Who burned your barn?"

"Wallace and the twins. They're Helen's brothers."

"Do they live here?"

"No, they have their own place over in Millbrook. They're a bunch of old bachelors, but not bad boys."

"Did you ask them to burn it down?"

"I did. I've been meaning to do it myself for a long time."

"Why today?"

He shrugged.

"I got sick and tired of looking at it, and the boys were down here visiting their sister, and they offered to do it. They're good with fire."

Mrs. Randolph re-entered the room and handed Annie the hiring papers. Annie looked them over quickly, carefully, then handed them back to the wife.

"I hope everything's in order?"

"They look fine, Mrs. Randolph," Annie assured her, "but I'd like to speak to the boy before I leave."

Jonas stood up.

"He's right outside. I'll call him in."

"That's all right," Annie said. "I'd like to speak to him alone."

There was no immediate response.

"That would be fine," Mrs. Randolph decided.

"Thank you," Annie said to both of them, "for your hospitality."

I stood up, we said our goodbyes, and we left.

Outside near the stables, we found Stephen Tyler. He seemed about my age, about fifteen, and he looked a bit worn out from his day in the field, yet very polite.

He explained that this was his third year with the Randolphs, that he'd never seen another boy on the farm, and that they'd always treated him well.

"When did you begin the harvest last summer?"

He didn't seem sure.

"It must have been August. Yeah, the middle of the month."

Which I knew was incorrect.

Soybeans are harvested in November.

Annie continued.

"You must have lost quite a lot of the farm's yield two years ago after the big flood."

"Yes, it was a very tough year, but they still paid me in full."

Annie thanked the kid, we mounted our horses, and we made our way off the Randolph farm.

With smoke, burn, and kerosene still wafting in the air.

23. Documents

Thursday, March 15, 1900

"It's *their* barn, ma'am. They can do what they want with it."

"Unless it's evidence," Annie pointed out.

For the second time today, Sheriff Bruckner was hoping that we'd go away and leave him alone.

We were standing in a little records room, adjacent to the sheriff's office, and, once again, we were pestering the sheriff about the Randolphs.

He didn't respond to the "evidence" remark. When he finally found the "Randolph" file in one of his cabinets, he opened it up and looked it over.

"There's nothing much here, just a record of the farm purchase back in 1873 and a copy of their marriage certificate."

"I'd like to take a look," Annie insisted.

Even though the sheriff's reluctance was obvious, he probably didn't want any kind of breach with another sheriff in another township. After all, they all needed to support each other and help each other out.

He laid the open file on the counter in front of Annie.

With me at her shoulder, we studied the two documents. Then Annie pointed down at the marriage certificate, at Helen Randolph's maiden name:

"Helen Langley."

I didn't say a word, and the sheriff didn't ask.

Annie closed the file and looked at the sheriff.

"We had a little unpleasantness earlier with Helen Randolph's brothers. Are they a problem?"

"Not really."

Evasively.

So Annie just stood there patiently and waited for more, and I believe that the sheriff believed that if he was ever going to get rid of us, he'd have to give her some information.

"Wallace Langley's not a bad sort, but I'd have to admit that the twins are a bit of a mess."

"Trouble?"

"Nothing much, some fights, some drunken stuff. Mostly they keep to themselves, and I'm good with that."

Annie was satisfied.

"Thank you for your time, sheriff. I much appreciate it, and I'm sure that Sheriff Granger will too."

"I've never met the man, but give him my regards."

"I will."

"You ladies have a nice trip back to Nutley."

It was, of course, a polite "good riddance."

"Thank you, sheriff."

As we headed for the door, Annie turned around and looked at the worn-out sheriff.

"By the way, when was the last serious flood in the area?"

He seemed pleased that it was a simple question of fact.

He thought it over.

"Back in the spring of '96."

Annie nodded, and soon enough we were outside at the hitching post and ready to mount. Earlier, at the Randolphs' house, I'd said next to nothing, and I'd said nothing at all during our two visits to the sheriff's office, but now, more than anything, I wanted to talk things over with Annie.

But I knew my curiosities would have to wait until we got back home. It was too late to catch the train, so we'd be riding all the way.

Nevertheless, I couldn't resist a single question:

"Maybe it was the Langley brothers who took Ethan. Right? Maybe they felt sorry for their childless sister?"

I felt ready to explode with endless questions.

"Maybe, my dear."

I laughed.

"That's all I get, Miss Annie?" I said with mock

frustration, which was, in actuality, full-blown frustration.

"For now, my dear. We'll have plenty of time at home."

We mounted our horses and headed back home.

Which is one of the nice things about a long ride, it gives you plenty of time to think things over, to ponder, to ruminate.

To detectivize.

24. Letter to Mr. Frank Butler

Thursday, March 15, 1900

Dearest,

This one, my love, will be short and sweet.

It's been a long day!

We found Ethan's barn, but it was burning to the ground. It was located out west in Hanover on a farm owned by a peculiar couple, Jonas and Helen Randolph. I have no doubt that they were covering their tracks and destroying useful evidence.

When we spoke with the Randolphs, they, of course, denied everything. They're quite an odd couple. I've never felt that the fact that you're ten years older than me was peculiar in any way, but "thirty years older" seems quite a gap. The wife's a pretty thirty-two-year-old, and her husband is a weathered old man, who, according to their marriage certificate, is now sixty-two. He also seems much too passive, too retiring, even too nice, to have done what was done a dozen years ago to Rebecca Miller.

Do I need to mention that I miss my husband? I'm delighted, of course, to hear that business is going so well.

You always, my dear, make everything go so smoothly.

Your loving Missie

25. James

Thursday, March 15, 1900

I was thinking about Jimmy.

I was wondering if one could actually love one's lifetime bang-around pal.

Once again, I was lying in my warm comfortable bed thinking about a young man.

A boy, really.

But I wasn't fantasizing.

I was remembering.

Remembering the night two years ago when we were so close.

Holding each other so close.

Dare I say intimately?

That night we were skating together, on and off, at the Cotton Mill Pond. It was very cold, but everyone on the ice kept moving, and no one seemed to mind. Jimmy, of course, was the quickest and best skater that any of us had ever seen. He was also the town's most natural athlete, and he took great pleasure in the fact that I was also known as a standout sportswoman, which allowed him to roughhouse a bit. To take certain liberties. To touch me and hold me in ways that were only acceptable within "sporting" circumstances.

Just being kids.

Just horsing around.

Throughout the night, he'd skate up to me from nowhere, take me by the arm, and spin me around on the ice. He would also hold me, and guide me, and twirl me, which I found perfectly exhilarating. Then he'd skate off again, in a sudden burst of speed, showing off for his friends.

But he always came back to me.

Later that night, when most of the skaters had gone home, he skated over, took hold of me, and we raced around the pond, laughing and swirling, until I finally lost my balance and the two of us slid off the ice into a huge bank of snow, falling all over each other. We were wearing leather gloves, thick winter coats, and warm woolen caps, but we could still feel each other closely. Right next to each other, and I could feel his warmth, his breath, and his care for me.

Something that was more than friendship.

Yes, we were just having fun, laughing at our mishap, rolling around in each other's arms, but I've never forgotten those wonderful moments when we held each other in the snow, and I suspect he's never forgotten them either.

It was my one-and-only approximate sense of the

special kind of intimacy that a man and a woman can have together.

Even though I was just a girl, and Jimmy was just a boy.

Now, more than two years later, I'm definitely becoming a young woman, suspended in some kind of strange transitional state, but Jimmy's still very much a little boy.

But he won't be forever.

No one else in this town, or anywhere else, not even Lawrence, has ever touched me, except for the formal dances at the Old Military Hall.

Is it possible that, someday, Jimmy and I might love each other?

That Jimmy might feel for me as Mr. Frank feels for Annie?

Who writes her love poems, which I've been privileged to read:

Love like ours, dearie,
Make the burdens light as air,
What if the storm assails us, dearie,
It passes in a while,
You and I together, dearie,
Will face the gale and smile.

Or such lovely thoughts as these:

Her presence would remind you

Of an angel in the skies.

I wish I knew my heart.

I suppose every woman feels this way sometimes, and I can't help wondering, if, on certain dark nights, before he falls off to sleep, James Edward Granger thinks, most fondly, of holding me closely in the winter snow?

26. Nut-ley

Friday, March 16, 1900

I previously referred to myself as "nobody from nowhere," but it would be more accurate to say that I'm nobody from *somewhere*.

That's because the location of my birth, my hometown, is a *very* special place.

(By the way, please ignore the precedent nocturnal cogitations. There must be something wrong with me!)

So what, to begin with, is "Nut-ley"?

As you might have guessed, it's a town named for nuts. Nut trees, in fact. In an older English, the word "ley" meant "field" or "meadow," and we all know what "nut" means.

It seems that the town got its name from the Nutley Manor House, built in 1828 on property filled with a wide variety of nut trees. Thus, the name, "Nutley." These days, the old manor house stands on the Satterfield estate, still flush with its tell-tale trees. As a matter of fact, the whole town has a preponderance of nut trees, and no one seems even slightly embarrassed by the fact that the name of their town comes from a bunch of nuts. As a matter of further fact, it's not uncommon for my Nutley neighbors to organize "nutting parties," and (or) "nutting picnics," along the Passaic River, picking nuts from all the nut trees.

Enough of that.

So, is the town called Franklin?

Or Nutley?

Nutley is actually part of Franklin Township, but it's been trying for years to legalize itself as its own entity. Thirteen years ago, the Postmaster General gave us our own postmark, and Mayor Langley expects the town to be independently recognized within a year or two.

"It's a done deal," he confidently assures anyone who asks.

I hope so. We'll see how long it takes the creaky wheels of the local, state, and federal governments to let us be who we want to be.

Nutley sits quietly at the foot of the Orange Mountains, on the west bank of the Passaic River, transversed by the Yantokah River, also known as the Third River, which empties into the Passaic. Our tree-lined, often canopied streets, with many wonderful ponds and parks and rolling hills, is, if I do say so myself, rather bucolic. Decidedly charming. As are our lovely homes, many of them (hundreds, in fact) having been designed by our distinguished architect, William

A. Lambert.

In its earliest days, given our access to Newark, Paterson, and Manhattan, Nutley (Franklin Township) began to create its own unique identity as a marvelous weekend retreat for New Yorkers, including many artists and writers. It was also exquisite horse country, and, in time, many of the weekenders moved here permanently.

Business, of course, as always, played a crucial role. A number of quarries of our high-quality brownstone flourished on the east side of the township, also known as Avondale, and a series of significant textile mills flourished as well. We're still proud of the fact that Essex Mills made countless blue-wool uniforms and blankets for our Union soldiers during the Civil War, but, eventually, sadly, both the quarries and the mills declined, although farming never did, mostly on the west side of town.

Does everyone love their town as much as me?

I don't know the answer to that.

Maybe being an orphan has something to do with it. Maybe I feel a deep and permanent gratitude to the little town that took care of me in my destitution.

Or maybe I was just lucky enough to be born and raised in such a lovely and interesting town:

With rivers, mountains, and scented peach orchards. With Kingsland Falls, Cotton Mill Pond, countless nut trees, the "Mile Stretch" (used every Sunday afternoon for horse-and-buggy races), Eaton

Stone's circus arenas, St Mary's Orphanage, and (maybe most important of all) P.F. Guthrie's confectionary store, where Annie often takes me for yummy homemade ice cream.

With trollies, trains, ferries, and riverboats.

With visits from President Ulysses S. Grant, Mark Twain, Thomas Edison, Buffalo Bill Cody, and many others.

With, every single marvelous day, Sr. Agnes, Dr. Carlyle, and Miss Annie Oakley!

27. Porch

Friday, March 16, 1900

"Tell me about my mother."

He shrugged.

What Miss Annie calls the "characteristic shrug." Mostly a shrug of the left shoulder.

We were sitting on the front porch of the Butler's home, a charming, three-story frame house, with a railed balcony, a five-sided alcove topped with a conical tower, a wide front porch, and, most important, located at 304 Grant Avenue, right next door to my own home with Dr. Carlyle.

At present, my father was still in Newark doctoring the injured, Mr. Frank was down in Philadelphia on business, and Miss Annie was inside her sportsman's room with two eager reporters from London. At least once a week, reporters from somewhere popped up in Nutley anxious to write an article of some kind about Annie Oakley. As you'd expect, she was always polite and hospitable, and the reporters, like everyone else, came away liking and admiring Annie even more than when they'd arrived.

I wondered if it was an unfair question.

After all, Ethan was only five years old at the time he was kidnapped, but I was still, maybe foolishly, hoping that that he might remember something.

Anything.

I'd spent most of the morning at the somber funeral and burial for Miss Jane Dalton. Mourning, like everyone else, and reflecting on the earthly finality of death, and, consequently, thinking about the mother I never knew.

Ethan, aware how much I wanted "something," did his best.

"I remember her scent," he remembered. "It was like the warm scent of roses. A comforting scent of roses. And I remember her voice."

"Tell me, Ethan."

"It was a very soft voice. A happy voice. One that always made me happy. I can remember her singing 'Clementine,' and 'Oh! Susanna' and 'Little Town of Bethlehem.'"

I tried to imagine my mother singing to Ethan.

Singing to me.

"But I can't remember anything else, Lizzie. I'm sorry."

It was lovely to hear him call me "Lizzie," rather than Elizabeth.

He looked at my hands. Actually, he was already

looking at my hands. Very seldom did he look anyone directly in the face, which made him seem excessively shy, which he was. He'd had so little human contact in his life that he didn't know how to behave with other people. Except to withdraw.

I felt that I could help him with that.

"I remember that bracelet, too."

He was staring at the small opal bracelet that was taken from the dead wrist of our mother twelve years ago. Eventually it made its way to the orphanage, to Sr. Agnes, who fitted it around my own little wrist.

I was three years old.

"You should wear this every day in honor of your mother."

Which I didn't fully understand at the time, but which I've worn every single day since.

Occasionally wearing her opal ring as well.

Sometimes her opal necklace.

I changed the subject.

"How are things at Lawrence's place?"

"Fine. He's very kind. Very encouraging."

"Have you had much time together?"

"Sometimes. Late at night. But being a deputy certainly takes a lot of his time. Especially with the sheriff gone."

"If you get too lonely, Ethan, you can come and live here. Or better yet, next door with me."

"I will. In time."

I tried to be delicate.

"Are you able to talk about what's happened to you?"

"Yes."

"Are you sure?"

"Yes."

I believed him.

"What was it like in that barn?

"It's hard to describe."

I waited.

"In the early years, I was alone and lonely most of the time, but I didn't really know what loneliness was. It was just how my life was. Every day. Every hour. I had no idea what it was like to have friends or brothers or sisters. Or go to school. Or go to church. I didn't even know such things existed. All that I knew was sitting alone in the mostly empty and darkish barn."

"Dark?"

"Yes, the only light was a bit of sunlight through the cracks in the roof."

"Did you try to escape?"

"Yes, but everything was locked and nailed. Besides, I was warned not to."

"Were you punished?"

"Not really. Mostly I did what I was told to do."

I found it hard to believe.

"Never?"

"There were a few times when I complained, then I wasn't fed, so I stopped."

"What did you do all day?"

"I sat on my bed in the darkness, humming my three songs, waiting for the woman to visit with lunch. With dinner. Which were the best parts of my day. What I lived for, in fact. She would sit beside me and hold me and comfort me and talk about the farm, and her house, and my father. Sometimes we sang songs together. Sometimes she brought me dessert. She was my entire life."

"Didn't you see her husband?"

"Not much when I was very young, but whenever he did come into the barn, he was very kind. Always asking if I was OK. Always asking if I needed anything."

"What did you ask for?"

"Little things. Silly things. Like more visits. More dessert. I didn't even know what to ask for."

It sounded horrible.

"Finally, when I was ten years old, he took me out to the fields. It was the most wonderful day of my life. My eyes burned from the sun, and later that night, after working beside him all day, I was terribly sore and completely exhausted, but I was so happy that I couldn't sleep."

Then I asked him the question I'd feared to ask.

"Did you love those people?"

He seemed surprised.

"Of course, very much. They were my entire world. I knew nothing else, and I wished for nothing more. Just their company. Their love. And helping on the farm."

I tried to establish some perspective.

"Do you understand, Ethan, what they did to our mother?"

"I do now, but I still find it hard to believe."

"Do you understand that, most likely, they'll end up in jail for what they've done?"

"Yes, but it's hard to imagine."

I wondered if I should stop, but I couldn't resist another question.

"Why did your father set you free?"

"I have no idea."

He seemed deeply hurt by the idea, by the abandonment, so I stopped with my questions.

We sat for a moment in the silence, looking down the tree-lined street in front of the house. Lovely Grant Avenue. Named for the legendary general and president who'd once visited Nutley in 1880.

"I know you were there yesterday," he said.

I was surprised.

Astonished.

Maybe Lawrence told him.

I couldn't deny it, but I wasn't sure what to do or what to say, and I wished that Annie was here.

"Tell me about it, Lizzie. I believe I have a right to know.

It was hard to disagree.

"We went to the farm."

"Did you see them?" he asked.

Eagerly.

"We did. It was a simple conversation."

"Did they ask about me?"

"No, they denied everything. They said that sometimes they would hire farmhands from the city. For planting and harvesting. Yesterday, they had a young boy on the farm named Stephen Tyler."

"That was *my* name!"

He was very upset.

"She said nothing about me?" he pressed.

"Nothing, Ethan, just denials."

He looked into my eyes.

"Was there really a boy there named Stephen Tyler?"

"Yes."

"Did you see him?"

"Yes. We spoke to him."

He looked away, crushed, distraught. I had the sense that he felt as though his life had been usurped. That he'd been replaced in the Randolphs' life. That he'd been rejected. That his entire past had been swept away. Eradicated.

I wanted to help, but I didn't know what to say.

"You can have a good life here, Ethan. With us."

It didn't provide much comfort.

I thought I should try and deflect his thoughts from the farm, from the Randolphs, from his past.

"Will you come to the game later this afternoon?"

He seemed disinterested.

"Please," I pressured him.

"I know nothing about the game."

"You can learn. It's fun! You can even learn to play. We'll show you how."

He shrugged.

"Please, Ethan, I'd like you to come."

He looked into my eyes a second time. It seemed that he wanted to please me.

"All right."

Then he stood up to leave.

"You're a good person, Elizabeth, and I know you're trying to help."

"That's what I want to do."

He believed me.

He nodded, stepped down the front steps, and walked up Grant Avenue. He seemed to me the loneliest person in the entire world, and my heart broke in terrible pieces. He seemed overwhelmed with all-consuming sadness, and I was concerned that his rejection by his "parents" and his usurpation by the new farmhand would transform his sadness into anger, into a desire for revenge of some kind.

I believed that he felt totally helpless.

So did I.

28. Baseball

Friday, March 16, 1900

It was more like "mudball" than baseball.

Yet no one seemed to mind.

Even though it had rained in the early afternoon, even though it was just a practice game, most of the town had turned out to root for the hometown Nutley Nuttters against our hated rivals, the Belleville Villains. Maybe the rivalry had intensified over the years due to inevitable and endless arguments over which team had the sillier nickname. Nonetheless, I'd have to admit that the boys from Belleville, despite their nickname, always seemed a decent and fun-loving lot.

Both towns, like most of the country, were daft on baseball, and most of us, fans and players alike, were ardent New York Giants fans, which had proved especially difficult last year when the team was 60-90, thus tenth place in the National League, thus 42 games behind the much-detested Brooklyn Superbas.

Yes, 1899 had been a horrible season to root for the New York Giants, but my own favorite player, George Davis, did his best to make things tolerable, batting .377, with 141 hits and 59 runs batted in. He was also, according to all the newspaper accounts, stellar at shortstop, always playing the game "fair and square." No dirty stuff. I say "according to the newspaper accounts," because I've never actually seen a professional game, but Dr. Carlyle has promised to take me to New York when the season starts.

It'll be an extremely interesting and exciting season since Mr. Ban Johnson's Western League, now calling itself the American League, is hoping to rival the National League by pilfering our players. The bidding war for the great Napoleon Lajoie has been discussed every single day in the newspapers.

What's next?

Irresistible payoffs to Cy Young, Honus Wagner, or Iron Joe McGinnity?

I hope not.

(Unless, of course, they end up playing for the Giants. Then I'd be forced to look the other way!)

The rain stopped about an hour ago, leaving the field a muddy mess. Before the first inning was over, the ball was hopelessly blackish-brown, and it was hard to follow its flight from the grandstands. I was sitting next to Annie, rooting for the local boys, especially Jimmy Granger, who, despite his age, beat out two bunts, stole two bases, advanced on a hit-and-run, and scored our only two runs. Given all the mud, the game proved to be a typical war of the "inside game," with many more bunt attempts than fly balls to the outfield.

After six innings, the game was called a tie.

No one complained.

The Villains went back to Belleville, but the Nutters hung around and played two more innings "just for the fun of it," even inviting Miss Annie to take a few swings, which she did, hitting a sharp liner past Jimmy at short for a stand-up single. Then Annie had a few words with Mayor Langley, who was coaching the Nutters (since Sheriff Granger was still out of town). Then the mayor waved at the stands toward me, and the Nutters allowed me to pinch run, but I was so excited I (moronically) got caught off the bag and tagged out in a rundown.

It was tremendous fun!

All of it.

Just the kind of community fun that dear Miss Jane had always loved, and both the day's practice and the Nutters upcoming season were dedicated to her memory by Mayor Langley.

Despite the good time, I must admit that much of the afternoon I was distracted, looking around for Ethan, who never showed up.

Even though Annie never mentioned my brother, she understood my concern.

"I'm sorry, my dear."

Where could he be?

Was he sitting inside Lawrence's little house, all alone, in silence? On the other hand, wasn't it possible that he was more content that way?

Or was he thinking about his "parents"? Was he plotting some kind of retribution? Or was it possible that he was actually longing to be with them again?

Craving their company?

I hoped not.

When the game was over and the crowd was mostly dispersed, I saw Lawrence riding up to the field in his deputy's uniform. Usually, Lawrence played a steady first base for the Nutters, but with the sheriff off in Newark, he'd been forced to miss the practice game.

He seemed quite serious, even from a distance.

Quickly, he found his father, and the mayor listened intently. Then Lawrence looked into the stands, saw Annie, and headed in our direction.

"Come along, sweetheart," Annie said.

We stood up and left the mostly deserted grandstands, meeting Lawrence behind the Nutters dugout.

He wasted no time.

"Judge Fairfax has been found dead in his living room. There's a suspicion of robbery. Mrs. Fairfax found him when she returned from the supply store. Fortunately, the boys have come home for the weekend."

The "boys" were the two Fairfax sons, Keith and

Bryan, both successful lawyers in Manhattan.

Annie thought it over.

"I'll go over there right away."

"Good," Lawrence said, "maybe I'll see you there later."

He hesitated a moment.

"There's something else."

We waited.

"Ethan's gone."

"When?" I blurted out.

"This morning. When I got up, he was gone, and so were all the clothes I'd given him."

"Anything else missing?" Annie asked.

"No."

"Are you thinking," I wondered out loud, "that *he's* the one who robbed the Fairfax house?"

I wouldn't allow myself to ask about the sudden death, maybe even murder, of Judge Fairfax.

"I don't know, Lizzie," Lawrence admitted.

Annie was calm.

"Let's not get ahead of ourselves."

It was hard not to.

29. Fairfax House

Friday, March 16, 1900

The Fairfax home was a beautiful Victorian on Franklin Avenue, with a wide verandah, two cupolas, stained-glass windows, with rather exquisite fretwork, featherboarding, and lace. It was painted a tasteful soft green, with dark green shutters, and it was, in my own opinion, one of the prettiest houses in Nutley.

A town full of pretty houses.

Miss Annie knocked on the front door beneath the stained-glass transom.

Keith Fairfax opened the door.

I really didn't know the brothers very well, so maybe I shouldn't have an opinion, but I'd always found them to be rather polite, but rather "stiff," even formalistic, even a bit standoffish. Maybe Manhattan had made them that way, or maybe it was all in my mind.

Keith was the older of the two brothers, in his mid-twenties, and, as always, impeccably dressed. In truth,

I'd always preferred Bryan, who was a year or two younger, and who also, just like his older brother, dressed in New York elegance. I was once told that they specialized in estate law, with a wealthy and sometimes famous clientele, and that they were highly successful.

But they never seemed as personable as their father, a kindly man who was now lying dead somewhere within the large house.

"Can I help in some way?" Annie offered.

Keith thought it over.

Briefly.

"Of course, Miss Annie, please come inside."

We stepped inside the high foyer.

"My mother's with Bryan in the living room, and our father rests in the study."

He felt it necessary to clarify.

"I believe there's been a misinformed report about a robbery, but nothing's been taken. My brother and I have been through the entire house, and even though I'm hardly trained in medical matters, I believe that my father had a failure of the heart. Or some kind of stroke. My mother found him all alone, slumped to the floor, and I've sent for Dr. Yorsten over in Belleville since Elizabeth's father is still in Newark."

I was greatly relieved.

There'd been no robbery. There'd been no assault or murder. I felt guilty, of course, feeling so relieved given that kindly Judge Fairfax was now lying dead in the next room.

But the relief passed quickly.

Where was Ethan?

Had he gone to Hanover?

For some kind of retribution?

More than anything, I wanted to talk to Miss Annie about it, but this was, obviously, neither the time nor the place.

Keith Fairfax led us into the living room, an exquisitely furnished room, as might be expected in the home of the county judge and his wealthy wife.

Mrs. Fairfax sat on the couch beside her youngest son, Bryan. She seemed simultaneously stunned and crushed. All her Fairfax reserve was gone. She was simply a disbelieving widow, mourning the sudden and inexplicable death of her longtime husband.

Bryan immediately stood up, bowed politely to Annie, then to me. Then the two brothers left us alone with their grieving mother.

Annie sat down next to Veronica Fairfax, took her hands in hers, and said nothing. There seemed to be nothing to say. I sat down in a nearby chair and did the same.

We sat there in the quiet for a while, and Annie's presence seemed to comfort the poor woman. But I was spending most of my time worrying about whatever Ethan might be up to and feeling guilty that I'd never been as fond of Mrs. Fairfax as the other ladies in Annie's circle. I feared that it might have been some kind of poor person's snobbery about the rich. But Annie was also rich. She made an astounding $1,000 a week with the Wild West Show. My father was also well-to-do, and, until two days ago, I'd believed that the Langley's were wealthy as well.

I'd always been instructed by Sr. Agnes to judge everyone equally, and I really don't believe that I've been unfair to Mrs. Fairfax. Maybe it was simply the fact that she often seemed less optimistic, less sanguine, than I preferred. Rather melancholic. Maybe as a consequence of her difficult and distressful miscarriage.

Annie stirred me from my ruminations.

"Is there anything I can do, Veronica?" she asked.

"Just being here is enough."

The sadness in her voice broke my heart. I wanted to put my arms around her and comfort her.

"But I think it's best," she continued, "if I lie down in my bed for a while."

She looked over at me for the first time.

"Maybe you and Lizzie could escort me to the bedroom?"

Mrs. Fairfax stood up, and we each took an arm, and we guided her to her bedroom. Annie pulled back the covers, and we helped her into the bed. Then Annie took off the exhausted woman's shoes and placed them neatly on the floor beside the bed.

"If you need me, Veronica," she said softly, "have one of your boys come and get me."

Mrs. Fairfax nodded with gratitude, and we

immediately left the room. After we'd re-crossed the living room, Annie continued right through the foyer, obviously heading for the study.

Which, I suppose, might have seemed a bit of an imposition, even an impertinence, but I was certain that Annie had her reasons, so I followed along.

Judge Owen Fairfax lay out on a leather couch still wearing his dark black suit. There was no blood anywhere, but the man's handsome features were now frozen in the paralytic grip of death. I was surprised that his lifeless eyes had been left open by his sons, and his eyes reminded me, of course, of the cold dead eyes I'd seen four days earlier on the banks of the Yantokah River.

Annie observed him closely, even taking time to examine his hands. Then she leaned over, placed her hands on his face, and looked inside his mouth.

I was astonished.

Suddenly, I was startled by a man's voice from directly behind me.

"I should have closed his eyes."

It was Keith Fairfax.

There was nothing in his voice that indicated any kind of displeasure that we'd come into the room without his permission or invitation. He seemed more concerned that his father did not appear in death as well as he might.

Annie turned around, as did I.

"He was a dear friend," she said, "and an

exceptional man. I'm sure you know that better than anyone."

"I do," Keith agreed. "It's hard to imagine life without my father's kindness."

It was a lovely tribute, and, of course, now I felt even guiltier for never liking Keith that much.

We left the study.

At the front door, Keith was equally magnanimous.

"Nothing could have comforted my mother more than having you here, Miss Annie," he said, then added, "and you too, Lizzie."

"Let me know if we can help," Annie said.

Then we exited the house of the dead and walked up Franklin Avenue in silence.

30. Bank

Friday, March 16, 1900

"I shouldn't be doing this, Annie," the mayor pointed out.

Which we knew was true.

"Especially today," he added.

Annie didn't falter.

"The sheriff would want us to know."

It was clear that Mayor Langley had no idea how to argue with that, so he didn't bother. He continued doing what he was doing, standing in his wood-paneled office at Franklin Trust, flipping through various bank ledgers, sometimes pausing to look, rather surprisingly, at what he'd found.

He looked up from his books.

"She definitely has her own account."

He seemed confused.

"A private account," he clarified for himself, as well as for Annie and me.

"Why would a married woman," he wondered,

"have a separate account from her husband?"

"You never knew about it?"

"Never, it was set up years ago, before I was chosen as the bank's director."

"When?"

He checked the books again.

"1890."

"Are you certain that it's separate from her business accounts at the supply store?"

"Yes."

"Then what's it for?"

"I don't know."

Annie waited for specifics.

"There's a deposit," he explained, "of $200 on the 15th of every month, and a check withdrawal in the same exact amount on the 22nd of every month."

"That' a lot of money, Warren," Annie pointed out.

"Yes, it is."

"Who makes the deposit?"

"I can't tell. Maybe Mrs. Fairfax herself."

"And the check?"

"It's made out to her two sons."

I must admit, it seemed perfectly reasonable that a wealthy woman might give a monthly stipend to her only two children, even though the amount seemed rather exorbitant.

But why would she keep it from her husband?

Was it possible that a wealthy woman like Veronica Fairfax was embezzling funds from her husband and then forwarding the money to her two adult sons, who, by all accounts, were highly successful New York City lawyers?

"Are you convinced," Annie continued, "that the judge had no knowledge of this account?"

"As far as I can tell, Annie," the mayor admitted, "but, who knows? Maybe he did know about it. There's no way I can be certain."

Annie went silent.

The mayor was frustrated.

"What's this all about, Annie?" he asked.

"I'm not sure myself."

Which wasn't much help.

Either for the mayor, or for me.

Then there was an interrupting knock at the door, and a familiar voice called out.

"It's Jimmy Granger, Mr. Mayor. I have a telegram for Miss Annie."

"Come in," the mayor called out.

Jimmy entered the room as he always did, with a contagious smile and high spirits. He nodded to the adults, handed the telegram to Annie, and looked at me.

"I stole those bases just for you, Lizzie," he said somewhat surreptitiously.

He often had a way of flustering me.

"Well, what if you did, Jimmy Granger?" I said, as non-committally as possible.

Annie finished reading the short telegram, then she looked at the mayor and explained.

"I asked Lawrence to telegram Sheriff Bruckner in Rockaway to see if Ethan was at the Randolph's farm."

We waited. She lifted the telegram.

"He hasn't been seen."

"Is that," the mayor wondered, "a good thing or a bad thing?"

"I'm not certain," Annie admitted, "but it's probably more better than not."

"Then where could he be?" I asked no one in particular.

Where was my brother?

What was he up to?

31. Letter to Mr. Frank Butler

Friday, March 16, 1900

Dearest,

Judge Fairfax died today.

Although unconfirmed, it seems to have been a failure of the heart. How strange that we should lose both Owen and Jane within a few days of each other. How strange that I never had the chance to talk to Owen about his relationship, whatever it might have been, with Rebecca Miller. Veronica, as you can imagine, is completely benumbed, attended to by her two sons.

No, you needn't rush home.

I know you still have important work to finish in Philadelphia, but I do long for next Wednesday when you'll finally return to Nutley and me.

Your loving Missie

P.S. I'll be traveling the next two days with Lizzie to New Brunswick and Manasquan, so I'll send you telegrams.

32. Rutgers

Saturday, March 17, 1900

Well, I wish *I* could go to Rutgers!

Just like my father did.

There've been many rumors and discussions about the establishment of a sister college, a ladies college, in conjunction with the Rutgers campus, but if it ever does come to fruition, it'll be too late for me.

But I don't want to misrepresent myself. I'm very eager to be heading off to Bryn Mawr in the fall, but wouldn't it be nice to attend the same school where my father first began his scientific and medical studies?

After several trains then a short carriage ride from New Brunswick station, Annie and I were now walking up the lovely green lawn in front of Queens Hall, the oldest building on campus, high on a hilltop over the Raritan, containing the college's administrative offices.

The building was designed by John McComb, the famous architect who designed New York's City Hall, Gracie Mansion, Castle Clinton, and a number of well-known lighthouses. Old Queens is a handsome brownstone in the Federal style, with Doric pilasters and a weather vaned cupola containing the Old Queens Bell, once donated by Colonel Henry Rutgers.

The name of both the bell and the building made perfect sense since the school had been originally chartered as Queen's College back in 1766, ten years before the Revolution.

Rutgers is the eighth oldest college in the United States, and there's lots of history here.

During the Revolution, as my father once explained, General Washington evacuated his troops across the Raritan River in 1776, as Alexander Hamilton and his New York Provincials fired artillery cover from his battery on this very hilltop at the pursuing British under Lord Cornwallis.

I glanced down at the Raritan as we entered the building, then we quickly found the Registrar's Office.

The assistant registrar, Miss Deborah Norris, a properish "all-business" lady in her mid-fifties, listened politely. She didn't seem to recognize Annie, which wasn't that surprising since we were dressed in everyday traveling clothes. Fortunately, Miss Norris had no problem with Annie's request. It was merely a reference check for a job application and not considered "privileged" information.

She left us waiting at the counter, retreating into the next room, a records room, then returned within a few efficient minutes.

"Nothing, Mrs. Butler," she said to Annie.

Annie didn't seem surprised, and neither was I.

"Which years did you check?" Annie wondered. "He claims to be twenty-four years old."

"*All* the years. *No one* by the name of Phillip Palmer has ever graduated from Rutgers, or even attended classes. I can assure you, ma'am, that the young man is obviously some kind of fraud."

Annie thanked her for her assistance, and we were soon out on the vast green lawn once again. We took a brief stroll of the campus: Van Nest Hall, Schanck Observatory, Geology Hall, Winants Hall, Kirkpatrick Chapel, etc. All the while, I tried to picture a young Dr. Carlyle rushing about the campus, to classes and laboratories, eager (as am I) for both instruction and knowledge.

Afterwards, we took our waiting carriage to the Brunswick Hotel on George Street, and soon after I'd settled into my rather lavish room, there was a knock at the door.

It was Annie.

It was too early for dinner, but it was clear that she wanted to talk, which was fine with me. We immediately settled into two comfortable upholstered chairs that faced each other.

"What does it mean?"

"I'm not sure, Lizzie. Not yet. Except that it's certain that the young man calling himself Phillip Palmer has entered into your home under false pretenses."

"You were suspicious right from the start," I pointed out."

"So were you, my dear."

I didn't disagree.

"Well, if you'd *really* taught McGuffey's for several years, you'd certainly know the contents."

"Exactly."

"But I must admit," I admitted, "he's quite a thoughtful and knowledgeable tutor. Even though his Greek's a bit ramshackled."

Annie laughed.

"The nuns taught you well."

"They did."

I had a question.

"I'm not quite sure why we needed to come down here? I'm very glad that we did, of course, and I'm loving our trip together and seeing my father's alma mater, but was it really necessary?"

"Maybe not, Lizzie, but you never know who you're dealing with in the mails."

I understood.

"Miss Norris certainly projects a competent air."

"Very much so."

There was a pause, a silence, then Annie altered the conversation.

"What do you know about Nome, Lizzie? And Dawson City?"

It seemed an odd question.

A non-sequitur.

"Only what I've read in the newspapers."

"Of course."

The gold rush in the Yukon and the subsequent gold rush to Nome had been covered extensively in all the newspapers, every single day for the past three years.

Sometime in 1897, after word leaked out of the Canadian Yukon that gold had been found near the Klondike River, an immediate migration of prospectors and miners flooded the area. Over 100,000 dreamers made the perilous trip over frigid seas and permafrost terrain and extremely difficult mountain routes like the Chilkoot Pass. Some got rich, most didn't, and the boom town of Dawson was immediately founded and immediately blossomed.

Then in late '98, word came down from the remote Alaskan village of Nome that the so-called "Three Lucky Swedes" (only two of whom were Swedish) had discovered gold at Anvil Creek. Unlike the Klondike, much of the gold was easily accessible, some actually found lying on the banks of the Snake River. Eventually, thousands of Klondikers rushed to Nome.

"Do you know where Nome is?" Annie wondered.

"Yes, western Alaska, near the Bering Sea. In the frozen middle of nowhere."

"Yes," Annie agreed, "I've been told that there's no real harbor there, and that the ships anchor off the coast and shuttle the 'gold rushers' ashore in boats, leaving them on the ice. Then they have to travel into Nome on dog sledges."

"It's a difficult way to make a fortune."

"And very few succeed."

But I was confused.

"I thought that the prospectors that you knew in the Wild West Show had done their 'gold rushing' back in the days of '49? During the California Gold Rush?"

"That's correct, Lizzie," she explained, "but last year, two young Klondikers were hired as stagehands. They'd come back from the gold rush emptyhanded, and they were extremely grateful to the Colonel for a steady job."

I was still confused.

"That's all rather fascinating, Miss Annie, but what's it got to do with anything? With Ethan? Or the deaths of Miss Jane or Judge Fairfax?"

"I'm not certain, my dear, but we can discuss it at dinner."

Which I was excited about.

I'd only eaten at a restaurant a few times in my life, always in Nutley, always with either my father or the Butlers or all of them together. But I'd never dined (and stayed) at a fancy hotel before!

33. Telegram to Mr. Frank Butler

Saturday, March 17, 1900

Dearest, Lizzie's tutor has lied about his education, and, I suspect, much more. We're now in New Brunswick where Lizzie and I just finished dinner. She's a marvel! Love, your Missie

34. Manasquan

Sunday, March 18, 1900

What words could I possibly conjure?

What descriptives?

What adjectivals?

Stupendous, vast, overwhelming, majestic, or terrifying?

I'd never seen the ocean before, its blue-gray endlessness, its depthlessness, its alluring terror.

I was standing after the Sunday service behind the little seaside church in Manasquan.

Earlier, when we'd arrived on the morning train from New Brunswick, the mayor of Manasquan was waiting for us at the station. Mr. Barton O'Brien had received Annie's telegram two days ago, and he was eager to both meet her and help her in any way that he could.

He'd also brought along a photographer, who was now taking pictures of Annie with the mayor, his wife, and other local notables. Even the minister asked for a photograph.

As always, Annie was polite and patient. I suppose she'd been photographed a million times, and by now, she was able to take it right in stride. Whatever the case, it allowed me a few moments to wander off by myself and stare at the ever-churning ocean beneath the infinite gray horizon.

What was I staring at, if I actually could see all the way across the Atlantic Ocean?

Ireland?

Portugal?

Morocco?

It was hard to believe that so many people, including my own ancestors, had managed to traverse such a frightful and incomprehensible ocean.

Later, when the parishioners were gone, we finally spoke alone with the mayor, who'd prepared himself properly.

"I've checked all the records," he assured us, "and I've done it *myself*."

"I appreciate your kindness."

He clearly appreciated Annie's appreciation.

"You found nothing?"

"Nothing," he said with confidence. "There was no such marriage between Warren and Frances Langley ever recorded here in Manasquan. As a matter of fact, there was no marriage ever recorded that involved either one of them."

Annie thought it over.

As for me, nothing seemed to make much sense.

"Is there anything else?" Annie wondered.

"Well, I do my best to avoid local gossip, Miss Annie."

He seemed sincere.

"It might be necessary," she assured him.

He understood.

"Well, my own mother, who was born and raised here, told me that there were once rumors about a child born out of wedlock in the Langley family, but she readily admitted that she didn't remember the family that well. Neither do I. Warren Langley left town when he was a young man, not long after his fiancée died."

"He was engaged?"

"Yes."

"To whom?"

"One of the Quinn sisters."

He struggled to remember her name.

Then it came.

"Suzanne. Yes, Suzanne, the younger sister."

Annie thought it over.

"Do you know where the older sister is?"

"Of course, she lives right here in town. She's now Loraine Kingsley, and she lives on the north side."

"Tell me about her."

He shrugged.

"She's a lovely person. A widow with two grown daughters, both of whom are married in the area."

"Could you direct us to her home?"

"Of course."

"I'll need to talk to her in private."

He understood.

"I'll have one of my boys drive you out to Loraine's. Afterwards, he'll take you to the station."

"That would be perfect. You've been very kind."

"My pleasure."

As we began walking towards the waiting carriage, I could see the minister waving enthusiastically from the front of his little oceanside church. His earlier sermon had been rather affecting, focusing on covetousness, specifically with regard to the ninth commandment, with a reminder of King David's illicit lust for Bathsheba, the wife of Uriah, one of his dedicated generals.

Which, of course, led to murder.

Then repentance.

35. Mrs. Kingsley

Sunday, March 18, 1900

"It was, I'd have to say, a rather frightening kind of love."

She hesitated.

She was having difficulty trying to characterize the intensity of their love.

"So passionate and so deep, seeming almost dangerous," she decided, "almost absurd."

She gave up, but we certainly got the idea.

We were sitting on the back verandah of Mrs. Kingsley's beach cottage facing the ocean, which like "love," is something that defies either description or explanation. She was very pretty, a carefully dressed woman, probably in her late forties, and her remembering eyes were gray like the sky and the ocean before us.

She was attempting to describe the passionate nature of the youthful romance between her younger sister, Suzanne, and Warren Langley. It happened twenty-six years ago, and I did my best to imagine our likeable, slightly portly, Nutley mayor as a young man caught in the conflagration of young love.

It was hard to picture.

"What happened?" Annie asked delicately.

"They were engaged and ridiculously happy. Then a few months before the wedding, Suzanne went for a swim, and she never came back from the water."

She pointed off to her left, down at the sandy beach.

"About a mile from here."

"Was her body recovered?"

"Yes."

Annie waited for more.

"After the burial, Warren came over to me at the cemetery, where we were all alone, and he told me that he'd taken a vow, what he called a 'permanent' vow, never to love anyone else again. Never to marry. A vow of celibacy. Naturally, I told him that my sister wouldn't want such a thing, but he was insistent and inconsolable, and I didn't try to dissuade him any further. We were both sunk in the deepest devastating sorrow. Sometimes I still am whenever I think of my dear sister, Suzanne."

She took Annie's hand.

"But I've had a good life, Miss Oakley, although sometimes when I look out at the ocean, I cry for whatever might have been."

Annie looked at me, then down at the little table in

front of us, so I poured some lemonade from the pitcher and handed the glass to Mrs. Kingsley.

"Thank you, my dear."

She took a little drink and smiled.

"My husband always loved my lemonade."

She reached over, poured the other two glasses, and gave them to her two guests.

I took a sip, and her husband was right.

Yum Yum.

"You've remained friends with Warren?" Annie prompted, somewhere between a statement and a question.

Mrs. Kingsley hesitated.

Finally, she decided to answer Annie's question.

"Yes."

"He comes to visit?" Annie continued.

"Yes, every few months or so, ever since my husband died, and especially since the girls moved away."

She clarified.

"We're friends, Miss Oakley. Nothing more."

That was that.

It was just that simple, and I believed her.

So much for all those "mistress" rumors in Nutley.

"What became of the illegitimate child?"

Stunned, I place my glass on the table, sitting, literally, on the edge of my seat.

Did Suzanne Quinn have a child?

The mayor's child?

"Very few people know about that," Mrs. Kingsley said evasively.

"I know that Warren's younger sister found herself in trouble."

I was stunned.

Re-stunned!

I never even knew the mayor *had* a sister.

Mrs. Kingsley thought it over a moment.

"I shouldn't speak of such things. I'm sure you can understand."

"I certainly do, but I need to know the answer to one question."

Mrs. Kingsley waited.

So did I.

"What happened to the man? The child's father?"

"He left town, and he was never heard from again."

"Are you certain?"

"Yes, he was nothing but a scoundrel, a low-life, and he abandoned the girl before Warren had a chance to run him off."

I was amazed, anxiously waiting for Annie to ask the next logical question, "Where's the sister?" And then the natural follow-up question, "Where's the child?"

But she didn't.

"Thank you," she said to the widow. "I know this hasn't been easy."

My heart sank, but I held my curious tongue.

"I believe that you've made it as comfortable as possible."

We rose and said our goodbyes, walked to the Mayor's waiting carriage, and headed for the station.

I was, of course, absolutely bursting with questions!

36. Stoneman Academy

Sunday, March 18, 1900

"I'm afraid I'm not at liberty to say anything about such things, Miss Oakley."

We were sitting in the director's office at Stoneman Academy in rural Linden, eleven miles south of Newark. It was quite an impressive place, looking to me like the kind of stone-constructed manor houses that I'd seen in English picture books, with a large circular forecourt, a steep shingled roof, high stone chimneys, and dark green ivy. Mr. Jackson's office was no less impressive, with a high wooden ceiling, a Tiffany or Tiffany-like chandelier, mahogany bookshelves neatly packed with handsome books, a huge mahogany desk sitting between him and the two of us, and mahogany everything else.

Outside the tall French windows, I could see the "wayward" boys off in the distance, dressed in their military uniforms, practicing their marching drills on the March-green lawns. This was the place where the wealthy sent the troublesome boys they couldn't handle, who needed to be forced back on the right and proper path. I was perfectly fine with the concept, as long as the disciple didn't metamorphize into something darker.

One certainly had the impression that such dark things never occurred at Stoneman Academy.

Earlier, to secure immediate access to the academy's director, Annie had announced herself as "Miss Annie Oakley," rather than "Mrs. Anne Butler," and it worked like a charm. Mr. Vernon Jackson was an exceedingly genteel, nicely dressed, white-haired man in his mid-fifties. His manners were impeccable, as was his desire to protect and preserve any academy information regarding former students and their families.

I wondered if we were at an impasse.

Annie took out a short handwritten list and methodically read off the past infractions and transgressions of the handsome young man who seemed to be in love with me.

Property damage, three times
Disturbance of the peace, five times
Perilous threat, twice
Public intoxication, various times
Threatening the use of a firearm, twice

"All before the age of fifteen," she added, "and I'm

sure that much more was covered up."

I was amazed, and, needless to say, greatly disappointed. When I was a young girl at the orphanage, I'd heard about Lawrence's reputation as a bit of a "bad" boy, but I had no idea that things had gotten so far out of hand. No wonder Fanny and the mayor had sent him here to Stoneman.

Mr. Jackson seemed unperturbed.

He'd listened to the listing without the slightest alteration of manner. As we waited for some kind of response, *any* response, I wondered if he'd ever speak again.

It came.

"Yes, the boy had problems."

Well, that was perfectly obvious!

I began to wonder if our stop here in Linden was an unfortunate waste of time.

"Any assaults?" Annie asked.

Once again, we entered into Mr. Jackson's "nothing" zone. He remained stationary in his seat, ramrod high, without the slightest movement of any kind.

I wondered if he was breathing.

"No," he said.

"Are you sure?"

"Yes, as far as I know."

"And you would know, correct?"

"Yes, unless, as you say, there was something omitted from his records."

"How long was Lawrence here?"

"Two years."

"I certainly understand your hesitancy to discuss his failings and his legal infractions, but I'd like to hear the other side of the story. The outcome of his stay at Stoneman."

"I'd be glad to," he said, clearly relieved.

Once again, we waited.

"Young Mr. Langley took to our methods immediately. He became a model student, always helping others. He was one of our most obvious success stories."

"Tell me more."

"There's not much more to tell. Whatever his youthful demons, they seemed far behind him by the time he left the academy. He was, and as far as I know, he still is, a quite remarkably hardworking and compassionate young man. I understand from his parents that he's become a respected deputy sheriff in the town of Nutley and a most positive force in the community."

Annie was satisfied.

But I have to admit, I still didn't know what to think.

After all, I've heard the many rumors that Lawrence Langley was hoping to marry me someday.

37. Hospital

Sunday, March 18, 1900

I ran down the long white corridor and fell into my father's arms.

He was taken by surprise, positively elated, and he held me tightly.

I'd missed him terribly during the last week or so, ever since the terrible train crash, but Annie and all our various Nutley mysteries had kept me preoccupied most of the time.

Every night, however, lying alone in bed, I would think of my father, dressed sharply in his medical whites, helping the victims of the train crash, and I'd feel overwhelmed with love and admiration and gratitude.

"I had no idea you were coming," he said to Miss Annie. "What a perfect surprise!"

"Where can we go, Matthew?" she wondered.

"The weather's lovely," he decided. "How about the outside deck?"

"Of course," Annie agreed.

Then she asked:

"Is it private?"

Which seemed like an odd question.

"I believe it is."

We walked quickly down several more hospital corridors, through the chemical and medical smells, passed rooms with numerous heavily bandaged patients. The crash had happened a quarter-of-a-mile before the main train station in Newark, being, according to the newspapers, the apparent result of the conductor's miscalculation. Five cars had derailed, twenty-two passengers had died either that night or soon afterward, and thirty-nine others were taken right here to St. Michael's, the largest hospital in Newark, with over three hundred beds. It was also where my father had served as Chief of Surgery before deciding a few years ago to concentrate on his expanding local practice in Nutley.

Naturally, on the first night of the crash, he'd been telegrammed by his colleagues at St. Michael's for assistance, and he was still assisting.

Ever since the death of Miss Jane at Centre Bridge, detectiving with Miss Annie had been a great and marvelous adventure, although, admittedly, sometimes a dangerous one, but *this* is where I wanted to be someday!

On High Street, at St. Michael's.

Nursing, curing, comforting.

The outside deck extended from the second floor, from the eastside of the hospital, facing the Passaic River. Which was the same New Jersey river that flowed past Nutley, eventually making its way to Newark, before emptying into Newark Bay.

Then Hudson Bay.

It was quite a sight.

Newark, of course, was a tremendous, busy, mostly industrial city, and even though I'd visited the hospital several times over the past three years – to help my father and to learn from my father – it was always nothing short of amazing to stand on the deck and look out over the great city and the great river.

I couldn't begin to imagine what New York City must be like.

We found several chairs at the far end of the mostly deserted deck, but before we sat down, Annie looked directly at my father.

She was strangely serious.

"I need to ask you about Irene Anderson."

My father, despite his natural reserve, seemed stunned, and I, of course, had no idea what was going on. I'd never even heard the woman's name before.

Who was Irene Anderson?

My father, always the gentleman, immediately regained his composure.

"That would be all right."

Annie nodded at me, yet spoke to my father.

"Should Lizzie leave?"

I felt terribly anxious, naturally fearful of missing something significant.

Once again, my father was momentarily conflicted, before making his decision.

"No," he said. "The truth is the truth, Annie. Please be seated."

We all sat down.

Even though I had no idea what was going on, there was something concerning about their demeanor. Even though Annie and my father were the best of friends, it made me apprehensive, even agitated.

"I mean no disrespect to Miriam," Annie assured my father. "You know how much I loved her."

"I do."

Miriam, of course, was the wonderful wife my father had lost to a never-clearly-diagnosed fever three years ago. I'd only met Miriam Carlyle a few times, and every time reaffirmed her reputation as a kindly and generous woman, being the perfect counterpoint to her husband. In 1893, when the Butlers moved to Nutley (right next door), Miriam and Annie had become fast friends, and I've often wondered if they might have discussed the fact that they were both in happy yet childless marriages. Whatever the case, not long after Miriam Carlyle's terrible death, Annie brought me over to the doctor's house, where he asked me if I'd like to be his daughter.

Two familyless people finding each other.

It was, of course, the most important and

wonderful day of my life.

Now I was sitting on the deck of St. Michael's and wondering who Irene Anderson might be.

So was Annie, but she was patient.

The doctor seemed to revert backwards, twenty-six years, within both his mind and his memories, as he calmly told us the story of his first love.

"She broke it off at the docks," he began.

We had no idea what he was talking about. Eventually, he went back to the very beginning and recollected his torrid romance with Irene Anderson.

They first met when my father was still at Rutgers. Irene was the only daughter of a distinguished family in New Brunswick, and she was, as my father put it, "a rare beauty." But she was also, apparently, lovely in other ways, having a kindly personality and a charming demeanor. Soon they were deeply in love, "fathoms deep," and she accepted his engagement offer during his last semester at Rutgers.

"At the time, I was buried beneath my studies, and, I suppose, insensitive to any alterations in our relationship."

Believing that nothing had changed, my father and his fiancée continued with their wedding plans, scheduled for the following fall after my father's return from a pre-arranged medical residence in London.

"But she broke it off at the docks," he repeated. "At the bottom of the gangway. She said that she was sorry, but that there was 'someone else,' and she apologized for her 'cowardice' in waiting for the day of my departure."

My father paused and remembered.

"I was devastated. I have no memory of ascending the gangway or boarding the ship. All that I can remember of that long ocean passage is nightmarish fevers, sweats, sleeplessness, and, if you'll both pardon the word, regurgitations. When the ship docked at Southampton, my mind gradually came back, and I determined to focus all my efforts on my medical training."

"What was the date of your departure?" Annie asked.

"January 10th, 1875."

"Are you certain?"

"I am."

"When did you return?"

"July of the same year. It was a six-months residence."

"Are you certain?"

"Absolutely. Yes. As a matter of fact, I still have my visas, tickets, and passports."

"What happened when you returned?"

"I never saw Irene again."

"Did you attempt to?"

"No."

"What became of her?"

"It's a rather unpleasant story."

"Tell me. Please."

He did.

"She became pregnant, and the man abandoned her."

I was horrified, but I said nothing.

"Then what happened?"

"I heard that her family did its best to cover things up and help her out. From what I heard, she moved out of state, but I never heard another word."

Then he made something perfectly clear.

"I never, of course, wished her any ill-will. Never."

"Of course."

"Soon afterwards, I met Miriam, and she swept it all away. All of it. But I'd never attempt to belittle those earlier feelings. I was very much in love with Irene. Fortunately for me, I was, later, even *more* in love with my dear most lovely Miriam."

It was a beautiful tribute.

"What was the other man's name?"

"I never knew. She didn't tell me that day at the docks, and I was too distraught to ask. Even if I had, I doubt she would have told me."

Annie seemed to know everything that she felt she *needed* to know, but my father was curious.

"Why is it important, Annie? Why now?"

"Can I tell you when you come back home?"

Unlike me, my father was in no rush.

"That would be fine."

"When will that be?"

"Most probably next Wednesday."

Annie smiled.

"Then it'll be a wonderful day! My own Frank is expecting to get back home from Philadelphia on the same day."

"Excellent! We'll celebrate!"

Then my father smiled at me, while still speaking to Annie.

"My daughter's told me that she'd like to try a small glass of sherry one of these days. Maybe that would be an opportune time."

Annie agreed, even though she never drank alcoholic beverages. Of any kind. Neither did Frank. They neither drank, nor smoked, nor cursed, nor gambled, and even though I was determined to avoid the last three, I have to admit, I was very curious about what a glass of sherry might taste like.

38. Telegram to Mr. Frank Butler

Sunday, March 18, 1900

Dearest, we're finally home again! There's much too much to tell, much of it is about love. I'll write tomorrow night. Love, Missie

39. Library

Monday, March 19, 1900

I didn't want to get out of bed.

I'd already disarmed the alarm.

I didn't care *what* time it was, but somebody was persistently knocking on the bedroom door.

I yanked up the covers, trying to ignore it. To be honest, I had no idea traveling was so exhausting. After only two days "on the road," I was worn out and sore. I didn't even know where I was.

I didn't care.

It occurred to me, briefly, that everyone at the orphanage would have been terribly embarrassed to learn that their best female athlete couldn't handle two measly days of riding a few trains around the state of New Jersey.

But I didn't care about that either.

Then somebody pulled away my warm and protective comforter.

I looked up.

Annie, ready-and-dressed for the day, smiled down at her weary tag-along.

"Up and ready, little Missie!"

I groaned.

"I'll get up. I promise."

"Your breakfast is waiting."

When Annie left the room, I realized where I was, in the Butlers' guest room.

So she could keep me close, protecting me from danger.

I lay back in my bed, my head comfortable on a feather pillow, looking at the ceiling.

Being Sherlock Holmes wasn't quite as easy as it seemed in the Doyle stories. Which were rather quickly resolved after a few clever deductions and a disguise or two.

Even serving as "Watson" was exceedingly difficult.

Pointlessly, I stared at the overhanging lamp and wondered what Miss Annie had in store for us today.

If I knew, I would have never gotten out of bed.

An hour later, we were back at the little library, in the tiny records room, inside Miss Dalton's house, which was now, oddly enough, the possession of Fanny Langley.

What were we doing?

Looking at documents again! Documents, documents, documents! This time, we were rummaging through the *old* documents, which comprised, in a sense, the entire legal history of Nutley (Franklin).

It was torture.

Annie did her best to keep us going, often kidding me from time to time, often insisting that we take breaks "to get a breath of fresh air."

Nevertheless, it was nothing but endlessly reading through repetitive documents recording land sales, home purchases, construction contracts, wills, births, deaths, etc.

"I wish I knew what we're looking for," I said rather wearily just before lunch.

"So do I," Annie admitted.

I caught myself about to shrug.

"You'll know it when you see it," she assured me, which wasn't much of an assurance.

Several times, when I felt like banging my head on the wooden table, I'd remind myself of the reasons that I was doing what I was doing. I'd think about the dead body of Judge Fairfax and the contorted dead body of Miss Jane, and I'd press forward.

Sometimes, out loud, I'd ask her dead spirit for assistance.

"Help me, Miss Jane!"

Annie smiled.

She seemed to think it was quite reasonable to seek otherworldly collaboration.

"Yes, dear Jane," Annie agreed, "please give poor little Lizzie immediate solace from her horrible labors in the Fifth Circle of hell."

I laughed.

Dante's Fifth Circle was for the angry, the wrathful, and the sullen.

"Am I really that sulky and gloomy?" I pouted. "I'm certainly not bad-tempered."

"Just a bit sulky."

"Never!"

She stopped and looked over at me directly.

"Actually, you're my dear helpful angel."

I didn't know what to say.

"Now keep reading!"

We laughed again and slogged on.

By four in the afternoon, even Annie had had enough.

"Have we learned anything at all?" I wondered.

"Nothing much," she admitted, "just a few confirmations."

Which was true.

We'd verified:

> That Warren Langley was definitely a first cousin to Helen Randolph, a significant fact he'd never bothered to mention.
>
> That there was no record of the Langley's marriage here in Nutley or anywhere else.
>
> That Judge Fairfax often took cash payments from his clients, which, although perfectly legal,

made the money difficult to trace.

But that was it.

I was quite discouraged.

"Don't be discouraged, my dear. We're making progress."

I controlled yet another urge to shrug.

There was a sudden knock at the door.

"We have a visitor," Annie said, so I stood up and opened the door for Theresa.

It must be odd to be so beautiful.

No matter *what* she was doing.

Whether practicing her archery skills, walking by the river, sitting on Annie's couch, or standing in front of me in the doorway.

She nodded politely, but she didn't smile her beautiful smile.

She seemed concerned about something.

"Come in, Theresa," I said, glad for any kind of distraction from the endless documents neatly piled and sorted around the room.

Theresa paid no attention to her surroundings, looking directly at Annie.

"I received your message," she said.

She sat down, directly across the table from Annie.

"Aaron will be here soon," Annie assured her.

Aaron?

Who was Aaron?

Theresa took it right in stride.

"I also saw Jimmy riding up," she added.

Which, likewise, made absolutely no sense.

Theresa, Jimmy, and somebody named Aaron?

Sure enough, a few moments later, Jimmy was rapping on the outside door and letting himself in.

He waved a telegram, nodded at both of the other women, then looked down at me.

"Hello, princess!"

"Hello, toad."

It was the best I could do, but he seemed to enjoy it, and he smiled.

Jimmy's smiles always had a way, as they say, of "lighting up the room," but, at the present moment, in our cramped and gloomy little room, any kind of smile seemed oddly out of place.

In the meantime, Annie quickly opened and read the telegram.

She thought it over, then looked at her Watson.

"It's from Sheriff Bruckner," she explained. "Jonas Randolph has been found shot to death. Two gunshots. His three brothers-in-law are being questioned."

All I could think about was my missing brother.

"No word of Ethan?"

"Nothing."

There was another knock at the door.

I was amazed.

Jimmy opened the door, and Phillip Palmer, dressed to the nines, stood waiting outside, looking as concerned as Theresa. He didn't bother to say, "I got your message, Miss Annie." It was perfectly clear that he'd been "summoned."

He entered the crowded little room and sat down in the only available empty chair, right next to Theresa.

As he did so, I remembered that Annie had carefully rearranged the chairs after lunch.

"Thank you, Jimmy," she said.

He smiled, ready to resume all his other responsibilities.

"Good day, Miss Annie! Good day to all!"

He nodded politely, then immediately exited the little library, as I sat in the ensuing silence waiting for I knew-not-what.

Annie looked at Phillip, wasting no time.

"Lizzie and I are fully aware that 'Phillip Palmer' is an imposture."

I felt privileged to be part of the team, but, of course, I had no idea what was going on.

When Phillip said nothing, Annie continued.

"I know that you're Aaron Anderson, the son of Irene Anderson."

I was stunned.

Phillip attempted no denial.

"Dr. Carlyle," Annie continued, "has told us, in detail, his history with your mother, and now I'd like to hear your own history. It's clear from your calloused hands that you haven't been working as a tutor. I've come to believe that you've been, until the last year or so, prospecting in Nome, Alaska, where you discovered enough gold for your fine clothes, your expensive gold watch, and your present imposture."

Nome!

Really?

Phillip was astonished, although, it seemed to me, less so than I was.

"What is it that you wish to know?" he asked respectfully, politely.

"I would like to hear your own history, Aaron, beginning at the beginning."

He debated a moment whether or not he should.

"You've always been kind, Miss Annie," he admitted.

"Then tell me the truth."

"I will."

So, he told us, in a rather calm straightforward manner the rough outlines of his life.

He was, he readily admitted, born out of wedlock to a "wonderful woman," who'd been seduced by a "despicable villain." To prevent her public humiliation, her family sent her to live with relatives in El Granada, a southern suburb of San Francisco, where Aaron was born and raised.

He seemed to have nothing but warm and affectionate memories of his mother who died five years ago, never having told him the full story concerning his birth.

"She refused to tell me who my father was," he explained. "I believe that she was fearful of what I might do."

"Meaning revenge?"

"Yes."

"Did you ever express any such inclination?"

"No, but she was fearful nevertheless."

My little heart jumped in my chest.

Did he think that *my* father was *his* father!

Is that why he'd insinuated himself into our lives?

And for what purpose?

"It'll be all right, my dear."

Annie had noticed my sudden anxiety.

"Maybe, Lizzie," she asked with concern, "you could use a breath of fresh air?"

It was an excellent suggestion, but I definitely didn't want to miss a thing.

Anything.

"I'm fine, Annie. Really."

When she seemed convinced, she turned back to Phillip, whom I guess I should start referring to as Aaron.

"Please continue," she said, so he continued.

"After her death, as I was going through her papers, I found a grouping of carefully preserved love letters written to my mother by Matthew Carlyle. Each was written before I was born. Naturally, I wanted to find the man, eventually becoming quite obsessed with the idea, but I had very limited resources. At the time, I was just finishing my studies at St. Ignatius College, focusing on English, French, Latin, elocution, and composition, and working part-time for the two de Young brothers at the *Chronicle*, which was, as always, in a bitter circulation war with Hearst and the *Examiner*. The *Examiner*, as you probably know, has always been far more 'yellow' than the *Chronicle*, far more sensational, but we did our best to keep up with things. Then the editor asked me if I'd like to go to the Klondike."

"Were you motivated by the gold?"

"Not at all," he insisted. "I know that might seem peculiar, but I saw it as more of an opportunity to build my reputation as a journalist, which might help me eventually secure a job back east."

"Where you could search for Matthew Carlyle?"

"Yes."

"So you went?"

"Yes, but things never work out as one expects."

No one argued with that.

"I secured passage on a ship to Seattle, but before I set sail for the Yukon coast, I heard a rumor about a new gold discovery in Alaska. About how 'three Swedes' had made a big strike, and that some people were actually finding gold nuggets lying on the shores of the Snake River."

He paused and remembered.

"It was the first time that I'd thought about the gold itself. But not, and maybe this sounds hard to believe, in a greedy kind of way. To me the gold, or the possibility of gold, was just a faster way to get myself to New Jersey. I had no illusions about becoming rich. And no interest. I was also fully aware that almost everyone who takes off on a gold rush invariably returns even worse off than when he'd arrived. Besides, I could still write the stories for the *Chronicle* that would enhance my career.

"So I sent a telegram to my editor and immediately set sail for Nome. I didn't even bother to wait for his answer because I was going to Alaska regardless, no matter what the *Chronicle* wanted. I won't bore you with the vicissitudes of the trip, but unsurprisingly I was the first real reporter on the scene. I began by interviewing Erik Lindblom and John Brynteson, two of the 'three Swedes,' but I soon became close friends with an old prospector named Damien Lewis, who taught me how to work a claim.

"So I did both. I panned and mined, not far from Anvil Creek, and I sent true yet fascinating stories back to San Francisco. Eventually, after about five months, I hit a small vein on a tributary of the Snake, packed up about two hundred and eighty-eight ounces, and returned to San Francisco. Then I quit my job and headed for the east coast.

"Finally, last year, I tracked down Dr. Carlyle, observing him from a careful distance at St. Michael's in Newark, then tracking him here to Nutley. By all accounts, he was a decent man and a dedicated professional, and I didn't want to simply knock on his front door, and say, 'I think you're my father, the man who abandoned my pregnant mother.'"

"So, you came up with the tutoring idea?" Annie said.

"Yes. Which I suppose was a pretty dumb idea."

He looked over at me.

"I hope you can forgive me, Elizabeth. You're a very bright young woman, and there were times in our few sessions together when I believed that you were tutoring me more than I was tutoring you."

I said nothing.

I still didn't know what the man was up to.

"Then on one of your surreptitious visits to Nutley," Annie said, "you met Theresa."

"Yes."

Aaron, very gently, took Theresa's left hand in his own and held it with affection.

They were lovers!

How could I have missed it?

Right under my nose!

Surely, I'm the world's worst detective!

"How did you know?" Aaron asked Annie.

"Oh, I've seen you two look at each other, and I've also seen you two trying *not* to look at each other. You've also been seen rendezvousing around town."

Aaron looked at Theresa, and they smiled at each other, and I would have thought it was perfectly lovely except that I still didn't know whether he was planning some kind of vengeance against my father.

"We've kept it a secret for over a year," Theresa

spoke for the first time. “It’s been quite difficult.”

“I’m sure,” Annie agreed.

Naturally, I assumed that they believed that either Aaron’s San Francisco relatives or his mother’s New Brunswick relatives, or both, wouldn’t approve of his marriage to a Lakota Indian.

Annie knew better.

She looked over at Theresa.

“You believe your parents won’t approve?”

“Yes. When I joined the Wild West show, that was my mother’s primary concern. That I’d marry someone from off the reservation.”

Annie understood.

“Maybe I could speak to your mother,” she suggested. “I know she’s a strong-willed woman, but I think that your grandfather would have approved.”

Her grandfather, of course, was Sitting Bull.

Theresa broke down.

Aaron put his arm around her, just like someday I hope someone will comfort me in my distress.

I’d never seen Theresa cry before. As a matter of fact, she never evidenced any of the more extreme emotions.

But this was powerful and real.

“I’m not sure it’ll help,” Annie warned.

“I have faith in you, Miss Annie,” Theresa said, as she quickly got control of herself.

Annie looked at Aaron.

“Are you aware that Dr. Carlyle is *not* your

father?"

"No, I assumed he was."

"What did you intend to do about it?"

"I really didn't know. I certainly didn't expect him to be the kind of man he is, but I still wanted to find out the truth."

"When were you born, Aaron?"

"November 13th, 1876, at St. Mary's Hospital in San Francisco."

"Are you certain?"

"Yes. I have my birth certificate."

"Which means that you were conceived in March of the previous year."

"Correct."

"But Dr. Carlyle was in Europe from January to July of that year. On a medical residency in London."

He was completely flustered.

"Then *who* was my father?"

"Exactly the man your mother said he was, the scoundrel who lured her away from Matthew Carlyle. Your mother broke off her relationship with Dr. Carlyle on the same day that he set sail for England. January 10th, 1875."

Aaron, obviously conflicted, thought it over.

"It was," Annie continued, "one of the most difficult days of his life."

Aaron understood, and he looked back at Annie.

"I'm sorry about all of this."

Which, of course, meant his own behavior.

"You should speak with the doctor," she advised. "He loved your mother in his youth, as I'm certain his letters revealed, and I feel confident that he'll gladly forgive her son's misguidance."

That seemed like a good word for it.

"Misguidance."

"I will," Aaron assured her. "I'll ask for his forgiveness."

He looked at me.

"And yours, Lizzie."

"You already have that, Aaron," I assured him, "but I guess I'll have to find another tutor."

Aaron laughed, and the others smiled.

I looked at Theresa.

"Congratulations, Theresa."

"It's very wonderful," she assured me, "to be in love."

"Yes, perfect," her fiancé agreed, as Annie nodded her approval.

I guess our long day in the little library wasn't as boring as I'd anticipated.

40. Wake

Monday, March 19, 1900

We left early.

Why?

Who wants to arrive early at a wake?

"I need to make a stop at the station," Annie explained, to my relief.

She pulled up the carriage at Nutley Station and handed me a handwritten sheet.

"Would you run this in and send it off?" she asked.

"Of course."

I looked at the sheet, went inside the train station, and telegrammed Annie's message to "Sheriff Richard Granger, Newark Police Headquarters, Newark, New Jersey":

"I'll meet your train at 8:05 AM, Anne B."

It wasn't much of a message, but I guess Miss Annie was planning to update the sheriff on our various adventures as soon as he arrived back in town. When I returned to the carriage, it was oddly empty. Looking around, I saw Miss Annie talking to a lean and tallish man on the train's platform. He was elderly, dressed in a black traveling suit, and quite serious. So was Annie. They conversed for a few minutes, then the man nodded politely, and Annie returned to the carriage.

"Who was that?" I wondered.

Annie hesitated.

"I've been very open with you, Lizzie, about everything, haven't I?"

"Yes, which I've much appreciated.

"Well, I'd like to keep this to myself," she explained. "At least, for now."

I sensed that, in some way, she was protecting me from something.

"I can wait, Annie," I assured her.

"Thank you, my dear."

A half mile later, we exited the carriage and entered the house of the dead.

The Fairfax House.

The foyer and the living room were crowded with mourners paying their respects. I knew most of the people from Nutley, but there were also numerous lawyers, clerks, and judges from the county's legal community.

Everything was terribly somber.

Judge Fairfax lay in the study.

We went there first to say a prayer, and his coffin

was closed, which surprised me a bit, but there was a large framed photograph of the judge displayed on top of the casket. He was wearing his dark judicial robes, and he looked quite handsome.

Eventually, we went into the living room and offered the appropriate condolences to Keith and Bryan and Mrs. Fairfax, who still seemed benumbed with shock. As we approached, Keith offered his seat on the couch, and Annie sat down beside the silent mourning widow.

Looking around the room, much to my relief, I saw an empty seat next to Theresa.

She looked as lovely as ever, even in black, and, despite the gravity of the occasion, I could sense her great relief that a personal burden had been lifted. Her love for Aaron was now public knowledge, at least here in Nutley.

I sat down, we traded hellos, then sat in the silent gloom of the moment. I couldn't stop recalling the famous Christina Rossetti poem, or, at least, its first four lines:

When I come to the end of the road
And the sun has set for me
I want no rites in a gloom-filled room.
Why cry for a soul set free?

Most of the people in the room seemed to be either discussing or reflecting on Judge Fairfax's many kindnesses, and I started thinking about his admirable kindness to my mother.

But I also tried not to dwell on the possibility that the dead man in the box in the next room might have been my father. That Keith and Bryan might be my brothers, my half-brothers.

Then I thought about the dead man hidden in his box.

"When I die," I said softly to Theresa, "I want a photograph, too."

Meaning a closed coffin.

She smiled her little smile.

"Me too."

41. Letter to Mr. Frank Butler

Monday, March 19, 1900

My dearest,

Phillip Palmer has acknowledged his imposture, which, in its resolution, has proven both harmless and rather romantic. I look forward to explaining in detail.

I've just come from the somber showing of our dear Owen Fairfax, which was not exactly a "showing" since the judge's coffin was closed. More on that on Wednesday.

Richard Granger is currently in Hammonton, of all places, having tracked down the apparently culpable conductor of the Newark train that crashed and derailed seven days ago, which I'm sure you've been following in the Philadelphia newspapers. On the night of the crash, Richard went to Newark to help his cousin, who, you might remember, is one of the city's police captains. When the conductor fled, there was a rumor that he had relatives in Hammonton, so they asked Richard to track him down. I've learned all this directly from Matthew and his telegrams, as he finishes up his service at St. Michael's Hospital.

I must admit that substituting for our always capable sheriff, and serving as his proxy, as his deputy, has been a difficult challenge in ways that I definitely hadn't anticipated. I've been forced, of necessity, to pry deeply into the lives of some of our dearest friends, uncovering long-sheltered secrets that I would, under normal circumstances, have no right to know. I've found the entire process terribly distressing, terribly disheartening, and I look forward to unburdening myself to you. I'm not, I'm certain you'll agree, that kind of prying busybody we both detest, and the only thing that keeps me moving forward in your absence is the terrible thought of the two murdered ladies. Miss Jane and Lizzie's mother. The one older yet still flush with life, and the other much younger one, with her whole life still before her. The one life taken seven days ago; the other life taken over a decade ago.

Whenever I'm not absorbed in my current "business," I'm thinking of you, my dear.

Only two more days!

Your loving Missie

42. Lawrence

Monday, March 19, 1900

I was sitting in Annie's living room.

Plotting.

It was about nine o'clock and dark outside. Theresa had already retired for the night, and so had Annie.

They're both early-to-bed early-to-rise types.

When I heard the horse approaching, I looked out at Grant Avenue through the curtains and threw on my shawl.

It was Lawrence, wearing his handsome dress uniform, sitting high on Jupiter, his black stallion. What young woman, or adolescent, or whatever I was, wouldn't like to see the likes of him coming up the street?

"Good evening, Liz."

He pulled up, dismounted, tethered Jupiter, and walked up the porch steps. I was waiting at the door.

"Annie wants to see me in the morning," he said,

even though it was nine o'clock at night.

I suppose the implication was that he wanted to talk to Annie tonight, but it also seemed like a pretense.

"Annie's gone to bed."

He didn't seem surprised.

"Oh," he said rather stupidly.

I smiled.

"You really came to see me."

He smiled as well.

"Maybe I did," he admitted. "Am I really that easy to read?"

"All men are," I declared.

Which wasn't exactly true.

After all, I hadn't been able to "read" my own tutor's love and affection for Theresa Morning Dove, even though it was perfectly obvious to Miss Annie.

Lawrence laughed.

"Could we sit for a bit?"

"Of course."

We sat down on the front porch swing, right next to each other, not quite touching. He'd dressed up nicely this evening, then rode over here just to see me, but now that he was here, he didn't have much to say.

We sat in silence.

I didn't mind. I was always comfortable with Lawrence.

"I'm going to miss you this fall."

I suppose that I hadn't really thought about it very much. About going away to college and actually missing people. I'd been so excited about matriculating at Bryn Mawr that I'd never fully considered the fact that I'd be missing everyone I cared for in Nutley.

Missing them, in fact, for quite a long time.

I didn't know how to respond.

Eventually, Lawrence turned and looked into my eyes.

"Were you shocked to learn about my past?"

He seemed quite worried about it.

In truth, he would have been *much* more concerned if he knew that I'd been to Stoneman Academy yesterday afternoon, sitting right next to Miss Annie as she read off his list of misdeeds and criminal infractions.

On the other hand, I also got to hear Mr. Jackson enthusiastically describe the "rehabilitated" Lawrence Langley, the one I knew and admired, the gentleman, the deputy, the young man of compassion and integrity.

"I *was* surprised, Lawrence," I admitted, "but I'm convinced that such behavior has been left in your past."

"It has, Lizzie, I assure you."

Maybe that's why he came tonight? To assure me that he was the good and decent young man I already believed him to be.

"Do college girls get married?"

I was stunned.

Had I, despite my earlier boastings about "reading" people, totally misread Lawrence?

Had I misread the purpose of his visit?

I was terrified.

Was Lawrence about to propose?

Right here on Miss Annie's front porch?

I suddenly remembered that warm night last June, right after the Summer Solstice Dance, when he drove me home in his father's carriage, and I thought that he was intending to kiss me on the mouth.

I'm sure that I would have liked it, but I definitely wasn't ready yet, which he must have apprehended, deciding against it.

Yes, I definitely wasn't ready back then, and I definitely wasn't ready right now. There was certainly a part of me that loved Jimmy Granger, and a part of me that loved Lawrence, but I really didn't fully understand love yet.

Not lifetime love.

Not marriage.

I wanted it, of course, but I didn't. I know that seems to make little sense, seemingly contradictory, but it actually makes *a lot* of sense. There's much in this life that we actively crave, for whatever reason, and which, for other significant reasons, we don't.

"It happens, Lawrence."

He thought it over.

"What about Jimmy?"

I knew, of course, exactly what he meant.

"What do you mean?"

"Do you have feelings for Jimmy? Feelings of

love?"

"Jimmy's only sixteen years old. Sixteen-year-old boys are like twelve-year-olds."

"That may be, Liz, but girls that are fifteen, like you, are more like twenty-year-olds."

I looked at him directly. He seemed especially handsome and appealing in the shadows of the moonlight.

"I'm still fifteen, Lawrence. Just fifteen."

He understood.

He thought it over and smiled.

"Well, I'm looking forward to when you're seventeen."

I smiled as well. Somehow, I'd managed to avoid hurting his feelings.

Lawrence stood up, and I did the same.

He stepped closer in the dark. I could sense his heat, his presence, and it felt rather wonderful.

Should I let him kiss me tonight?

I had no idea.

He looked directly into my eyes.

Deep.

"Someday, I'd like to kiss Miss Elizabeth Miller."

"I'd like that, too," I admitted. Then I recovered and added, "Someday."

Lawrence opened the front door, and I stepped back into the house.

Had I behaved properly?

Had I done things properly?

Had I been unkind in any way?

Or, equally dangerous, had I somehow led him on? Had I made some kind of compact, some kind of commitment?

I was totally conflicted.

The truth is, it's not easy being a young woman.

There are no guidelines. The writings of Miss Austen are helpful, but, in truth, every young girl like me, moving maybe much too quickly into womanhood, is entirely on her own, with nothing but her good sense to guide her.

I wondered what I'd be thinking about if I'd let him kiss me?

I pushed it from my mind, went into the kitchen, and wrote the note that I'd been plotting when Lawrence rode up the street to visit me.

> *Dearest Annie, I must have upset my stomach at dinner. A warm glass of milk has helped a bit, but I think some rest is needed. I plan to turn off my alarm for the morning, but, of course, if you need me for anything, just come into the room and wake me up. Love, Lizzie*

I placed the note on the kitchen table.

I've always prided myself on truthfulness, finding prevarication positively anathema, so I was, of course, ashamed of myself and my present machinations.

But they were necessary.

Does the seeming "necessity" of a lie, I wondered, transform it into something less than a lie?

Since I knew the answer, I refused to ponder my own interrogative, and I went to bed.

43. Hanover

Tuesday, March 20, 1900

When I heard her coming, I mounted Adler.

Since the hoofbeats indicated a single rider, I was rather confused.

Earlier, before sunrise, I woke myself, dressed, and left another note on the top of my bed.

Just in case my anticipations were incorrect.

Just in case Annie decided to come into the bedroom.

> *Dear Miss Annie, I've gone to Hanover, waiting to accompany you. Please don't be angry. Love, Elizabeth.*

Last night, I was certain that Annie was planning to go to Hanover without me, planning to confront and possibly arrest Mrs. Randolph, and I naturally assumed that she was intending to bring Lawrence along. I knew, without a doubt, that she'd refuse to allow me to come, so I wrote my note full of lies to mislead her. Then I got up even earlier than Annie, making the long ride on Adler to the narrow dirt road that led to the Randolph farmhouse.

As Annie approached, I pulled Adler out to the road.

Annie stopped and looked at me directly.

I wondered if she'd dress me down. She'd never, in all the years we'd known each other, been angry at me before, but this was different.

I'd lied.

Fortunately, she smiled.

"You're a naughty girl," she said.

"And you were planning to go without telling me," I pointed out.

"Yes, for your own protection, my dear."

"Well, I'm here now," I said, as if it were fait accompli.

"Well, little Missie, you can wait right there in your hiding place until I get back."

"I'm coming with you, Annie."

"It could be dangerous, Lizzie."

"If it is, I've got my Winchester 92, and I've been instructed by the best marksman in the entire world."

It was a gift from Annie and Frank:

Winchester Repeating Arms, 32-20 rifle, 1892, lever action, blued tapered octagon barrel, adjustable rear sight, blade front sight, excellent bore, walnut butt stock.

She shook her head, in spite of herself, and laughed.

But I was still serious.

"He's my brother, Annie. And that woman probably killed my mother."

She thought it over, but the truth is, she realized that she had no choice.

"All right," she finally gave in, "but do as I say. *Exactly* as I say."

"I will. I promise."

She looked at me with both concern and affection.

"If anything happens to you, it'll destroy your father."

"I know."

She believed me.

Then we headed up the sloping road to the burned-out barn, dismounted, tied the horses, and pulled our rifles.

"I thought Lawrence was coming," I wondered.

"I sent him to Belleville."

Of course, she did. She wanted to protect Lawrence in the same way that she wanted to protect me.

"I want you to walk behind me, at least eight paces behind, and keep a close eye on the surrounding trees, for possible cover if we need it."

I understood and nodded as we continued up the

narrow road towards the little log cabin. There was no one around. No movement. No sound.

It felt unnatural.

About fifty feet from the front door, Annie stopped next to the trunk of a sizable oak and looked back at me.

Quickly, I found an oak of my own.

"Helen Randolph!" she called out. "It's Anne Butler. We need to talk."

There was no response.

Nothing.

Since we were both somewhat exposed, I was afraid that someone might fire from within the house.

There was a sudden sound inside the cabin.

Immediately, Annie fired through the front window, hitting it high on the glass and crashing it down to the ground in shattered pieces. It made quite a racket, and now we could see directly into the Randolph living room.

It was empty.

Then I noticed that someone with a shotgun was standing outside, at the far right-hand corner of the house. It was Mrs. Randolph, and she was lifting the barrel of her Parker 12-guage directly at Annie.

Her intentions were clear.

I lifted my Winchester, but Annie had also seen her, and she fired instantly.

Mrs. Randolph was struck in the left thigh, and she collapsed to the ground in a heap, clutching at her leg.

Then I saw Ethan.

He was approaching from behind us, off to our right, far behind Miss Annie, outside her line of vision.

He'd seen his "mother" crumple to the ground, and he was terrified.

He was also enraged.

When he saw Annie, he immediately lifted his Remington, fully intending to shoot her in the back.

I didn't hesitate.

I sighted my Winchester and fired, hitting my brother in the left shoulder. He dropped his weapon, stared momentarily at his shoulder, and then, despite the pain and the injury, he rushed forward to comfort his wounded mother.

As Annie and I stepped forward, Ethan fell over his whimpering mother, wrapping his arms around her protectively, and crying with fear and rage.

"You'll be all right!" he kept saying, over and over.

Then he looked up at Annie and me.

"I'll kill you both!"

Then he kissed Helen on the forehead several times.

Then he kissed her on the mouth.

What!

44. Sheriff

Tuesday, March 20, 1900

"I'm sorry I wasn't much help."

I felt like saying, "You weren't any help at all!" but I held my tongue.

So did Miss Annie.

At least the man was "man enough" to apologize.

He stood about six-feet high, a full foot taller than Annie, but he seemed much smaller and far less significant than the little lady who'd brought in the murderer, as well as the attempted murderer.

My own brother.

Who was sitting in the next room, inside the sheriff's jail cell, unaware that Helen Randolph had been taken to the infirmary under guard.

Not that her wounds were any more serious than Ethan's, but the sheriff wisely wanted to keep them apart until he had a chance to interrogate them separately.

Fortunately, neither of the wounds was serious. My

.32 WCF bullet had struck Ethan in his left shoulder and come out his back rather cleanly. The woman's wound in her thigh had been shot, as one might expect, rather expertly by Miss Annie, missing both bones and arteries.

How my own shot at Ethan was so well-placed is beyond me. I suspect that the fact that I had no time to panic helped quite a bit. I also had the feeling that my hands were guided by our mother, helping me to incapacitate her wayward child, while simultaneously preventing her daughter from seriously wounding her own brother.

Earlier, after he'd kissed his mother on the mouth, Ethan looked up at me.

Full of venom.

"I hate you!"

He said it in a way that left me momentarily damaged and paralyzed.

Then he actually lunged at Annie, but she was remarkably unperturbed. She pushed him back down to the ground with the butt of her Marlin '91, then stood her ground, right above both Ethan and Helen Randolph.

"Your mother needs attention," she said.

I was, of course, surprised by the word "mother," but it seemed to calm Ethan down. Kneeling in the dirt, he fell back protectively over the woman who'd once abducted him.

Then Annie went about her business.

She walked back to Gypsy, pulled a cloth bag from her satchel, and came back to Ethan.

"Stand up."

He stood up.

"Let me see it," she said.

She opened his shirt to look at the bleeding wound.

"Do her first!" he said.

Annie ignored him.

"Turn around," she said.

Ethan did as he was told.

She quickly bound his hands behind his back.

"Now sit down, right over there."

When she pointed at the ground, Ethan sat down and watched as Annie cut away Helen's cotton breeches and looked at her wound.

The woman had stopped sobbing, but she said nothing.

What was there to say?

Annie looked over at Ethan.

"It's not serious."

His relief was obvious and immediate. He almost seemed human again.

Satisfied, Annie looked at me.

I was standing there with my weapon ready, hoping that I'd never have to use it again.

"We'll need to take them in, Lizzie."

I got the message.

As Annie continued to bind up the woman's leg, I went inside the stable and returned with the two best mounts.

Eventually, after Ethan was also patched up, we helped him on one of the horses, then did the same for Mrs. Randolph. It was a slow and tedious ride to Rockaway and the sheriff's office, and even though I had little respect for the man, I was glad that he was there.

"You were right?" he asked Annie.

"We were."

That was that.

There was no argument.

Immediately, he took charge of the two prisoners, determined to keep them apart.

"She's ready to talk," Annie said. "She knows it's over, and she'll want to protect the boy."

He nodded.

"What about him?"

"He'll probably keep silent."

Annie looked at the hulking sheriff.

"I'd greatly appreciate knowing the outcome."

"Of course," he assured her. "If they talk tonight, I'll send you a report in the morning."

He seemed eager, even solicitous, and I had no reason to doubt either his competency or his efficiency.

Annie was satisfied.

Later, when it was time to leave, I looked at the sheriff.

"I'd like to see him again."

"Of course."

"Just *see* him," I clarified.

He understood, leading me and Annie into a small side room where we could see Ethan in the distance, but he couldn't see us.

He was sitting on a small wooden bench, looking very much as I'd first seen him in the Nutley jail cell, staring down at the ground.

This time he was crying.

It broke my heart.

I walked out of the room, out of the office, to the hitching post and the horses.

Annie was concerned.

"Are you all right, my dear?"

"I'd like to go home."

"Me too."

We mounted in silence and began the long ride back to Nutley.

45. Telegram to Mr. Frank Butler

Tuesday, March 20, 1900

Dearest, Helen Randolph has been arrested. Ethan as well. Tomorrow will be the best day of the year! I'll meet you at the station at 9:16 AM Love, Missie

46. Report

Wednesday, March 21, 1900

The courier arrived at 9:35.

It wasn't Jimmy, and I was grateful. I knew what was waiting inside the envelope. Sheriff Bruckner's report to Miss Annie, who, at the moment, was off at the Nutley Station waiting for her love to return from Philadelphia.

"Can I read it if it comes while you're gone?"

She didn't hesitate.

"Of course, my dear. But it might be difficult."

"I know."

We were just finishing breakfast, and we were still sitting at the kitchen table. Annie was planning to go to the station to meet with Sheriff Granger.

"You can come if you'd like," she offered.

"I'll wait."

We both knew what that meant. I was so obsessed with my brother's situation that I preferred to wait right here in the hope that the report would arrive this morning before the funeral.

For Judge Fairfax.

Over the course of the past nine days, Annie and I had been exposed to all kinds of secret, peculiar, human behaviors, and we, in turn, had always discussed them as adults might discuss such things.

But there was one thing that remained unsaid.

Which was much too uncomfortable.

So, I said it.

Or asked.

"They were lovers."

Annie was not unprepared.

"It seems they were."

I tried to fathom such a possibility.

"We need to remind ourselves, Lizzie, that she wasn't *really* his mother."

Rather deftly, she'd avoided using the word "incest."

"I know. But Ethan's only seventeen, and, according to her marriage certificate, she's now thirty-two."

Annie said nothing.

"Besides," I continued, "we have no idea when it started."

That was a particularly ugly thought, and there was, yet again, another silence.

"Ethan," she reminded me, "was her captive, her prisoner. For his entire life. You and I can't possibly comprehend such a thing. He was *totally* dependent on her for sustenance, for companionship, for human interaction."

That, as we both knew, was the best possible defense that might be offered on Ethan's behalf.

A defense of the indefensible.

"But he *had* to know," I pressed forward, "that he was betraying the man whom he believed was his father."

"Yes," she agreed.

Annie looked across the table.

"Are you sure you want to read the report?"

I shrugged.

Now I was holding the thing in my hands.

At the moment, I was waiting for Theresa to come down from her room, so we could wait together for Aaron to arrive and take us to the funeral.

I wondered if I had enough time.

Sitting down on the couch in the living room, I didn't hesitate, quickly opening the envelope and reading the sheriff's attached note:

Dear Mrs. Butler,

Enclosed forthwith is a brief account of my interrogation of Mrs. Randolph. As you'd anticipated, the boy has maintained his silence. In a few days, I'll forward you a more thorough account. Again, I do hope you can forgive my thickheadedness. You've made me realize that even though a hardworking family keeps to itself and doesn't cause trouble, that doesn't mean that they might not have broken or still be breaking the law.

With much respect, Sheriff Jason Bruckner

It was neatly written in black ink in a distinctive hand that employed both script and printed letters. The attached report, a single page, was written in the same manner:

Statement from Mrs. Helen Randolph, March 21, 1900, conducted at the prisoner's bedside, Riverton Infirmary, Morristown, State of New Jersey, by Sheriff Jason Bruckner.

Mrs. R. admits to the murder of Mrs. Rebecca Miller, with three gunshots on the banks of the Passaic River in Franklin Township on March 12, 1888. She also admits to the abduction of the dead woman's five-year-old son, Ethan Miller, which was the motivation for the murder. ("My husband was too old to have children.") Said husband, Jonas Randolph, was, according to Mrs. R., entirely unaware of either the homicide or the kidnapping. ("I told him that the child was recently orphaned, and he believed me.")

For five years, the boy, renamed Stephen Tyler, was confined to a storage barn and hidden from the public. At the age of ten, he began working the farm, as a so-called "hired farmhand" with his father. In time (three years ago), Mrs. R. initiated a sexual relationship with Ethan Miller. (I can only record what I've been told.) Two weeks ago, Mr. Randolph discovered the carnal assignations of his wife and his son, and he took the boy ("while I was asleep") and abandoned him in upstate New York. ("I won't begin to describe the hatred I had for him for that. But I knew that my Stephen would come back to me as soon as he was able.") When he did so, Mrs. R. shot Mr. R. with the same shotgun she'd used in the earlier killing.

(Note: Mrs. R.'s three brothers, Wallace, Lewis and Brooks Langley of Millbrook, the previously presumed suspects in the murder, have now been released from confinement.)

Mrs. R. seems to have no regrets, except for the uncertain fate of Ethan Miller, who attempted to murder Mrs. Anne Butler on the day of his arrest.

It was signed, "Jason Bruckner."

I placed the report on the couch beside me. It was a lot for a young girl to unpack.

47. Fanny

Wednesday, March 21, 1900

I rushed next door.

It was three o'clock in the afternoon, and I was bursting with curiosities.

My father had arrived on the noon train, excited to be back home, but disappointed that he'd missed the burial.

"Owen was a good man," he said, as if to himself. "He was a good friend."

We didn't linger long on the death of his friend. We carriaged back home and spent three wonderful hours together. He wanted to hear about my adventures with Miss Annie, and I wanted to hear about his work at the hospital. Modest as always, he made light of his service at St. Michael's, saving the lives of many of the victims of the terrible train crash.

I did get him to admit that he'd performed over thirty surgeries.

"I wish I was there to help," I said.

It was true.

My time with Annie "detectivizing" had been amazing, but we all knew that nursing was my chosen profession.

We talked for hours.

"I suppose I should unpack," he said eventually, "and change for the get-together."

"Of course," I said. "Can I go next door and help the Butlers prepare?"

He smiled.

"You're dying to interrogate Miss Annie."

"Is it *that* obvious?"

"Yes, and perfectly natural."

The truth was, I hadn't been alone with Annie since breakfast. She'd gone off to meet the sheriff at the early morning train, then she did who-knows-what? before returning to the station to meet her dear Frank on the 9:16 train. Then they went directly to the funeral and the burial.

Then it was *my* turn to go to the station, to meet the father I'd missed so much. Now it was three o'clock in the afternoon, an hour before the planned get-together at Miss Annie's, which I'm sure she wasn't really looking forward to. As for Mrs. Fairfax, she was much too distraught after the burial to do anything but go home to bed, and her family had decided to postpone the judge's memorial reception until tomorrow evening.

As mentioned earlier, I rushed next door, knocked, and immediately entered. Annie and Mr. Frank were arranging chairs in the living room.

"Can I help?"

The more I helped, the quicker things would be readied, and the more time I'd have with Annie before the "explanations" began.

The doorbell rang.

My heart sank.

I wished whoever it was would go away.

"Would you get that, my dear?" Annie asked.

I went to the front door, wishing that when I opened it there'd be nobody there.

It was Fanny and the mayor.

"Did they," I wondered to myself, "get the time wrong?"

"We've come early," Fanny admitted, rather awkwardly.

As a matter of fact, they both seemed nothing but awkward, which was definitely not normal for either one of them.

"Is Annie available?" the mayor asked.

Which also seemed rather odd.

"Of course," I assured them. "Come in."

They didn't move.

"We'll wait," Fanny said.

Then I sensed a presence behind me as Annie came to the rescue.

"Hello, come inside!"

They held their ground.

"We've had a note from Loraine Kingsley," the

mayor explained. "Could we talk out here, Annie? I know you're busy."

Annie was unperturbed.

"Of course."

She grabbed a shawl off the coat rack, stepped onto the porch, as did I, then she shut the door behind us. She gestured to the Langleys, who sat together on the front porch swing, as if riding in the cart on the way to the guillotine.

Annie and I took nearby seats, and I was very grateful that no one asked me to leave.

Besides, I already knew much of what Annie knew.

The mayor didn't waste any time.

"She says that you *know*."

"She," of course, meant Mrs. Kingsley of Manasquan.

"I do," Annie admitted. "And I'm sorry that I felt it was necessary to do so."

Neither of them seemed to blame Annie.

"You were just doing what the sheriff asked you to do."

"I was," Annie agreed, "and there were several facts that seemed to necessitate looking into your past."

"My argument with Miss Jane," the mayor admitted.

"Yes, and the fact that Lawrence was actually born in New Castle, Pennsylvania."

Which they'd lied about, but Annie, politely,

refrained from using the word “lie.”

“There was something else,” Annie continued. “The fact that you’re related to Helen Randolph.”

They were both astonished and looked at each other.

Annie clarified.

“Her maiden name was Helen Langley. She’s your paternal first cousin.”

“I’ve never even heard of her,” the mayor explained. “I’ve got cousins in Eastern Pennsylvania, but I never knew of anyone in Hanover.”

He was quite convincing, and Annie seemed convinced as well.

Now that the prelude was over, there was a momentary silence.

The mayor looked at Annie.

“Could you tell us what you know?”

“I know that Fanny is your sister.”

What!

I was stunned.

The Langleys said nothing, waiting for more.

Annie continued.

“Mrs. Kingsley told us of your passionate love for Suzanne Quinn, her tragic death in the ocean, and your vow of perpetual devotion and celibacy. Around that time, Fanny, your younger sister, who was born Catherine ‘Cathy’ Langley found herself pregnant and abandoned, and I believed you offered her a way to ‘start over in life.’ You left Manasquan together, changed Fanny's name, pretended to be married, and raised Lawrence as your own child."

Whoa!

I'll definitely need some time to acclimate myself to that!

"I've maintained my vow," the mayor assured us.

"We've always been very comfortable with each other," Fanny pointed out. "Sometimes a married couple can be so close and caring that they seem like a brother and a sister."

I'd have to ponder that one too.

There was another brief silence.

The mayor looked at Annie and got to the purpose of the visit.

"What's to be done?"

She didn't hesitate.

"Nothing."

Their relief was visible, palpable.

"Nothing at all?" he asked.

"Nothing."

"It stays with you?"

"Yes, and with Lizzie."

Fanny was overcome with emotions.

"You're a true and dear friend, Annie."

The mayor stood up and helped his sister from the porch swing.

"We'll come back later," he said, "when the others arrive."

"There's no need for that, Warren," Annie

suggested. “Why not come in right now?”

Which, of course, meant I’d never get a moment alone with Annie.

But Fanny had a final question.

“What about Lawrence?” she wondered. “Should we tell him?”

“That would be up to you,” Annie assured them.

“What do you suggest?” the mayor asked.

“The truth.”

To Annie, it was that simple, but it was also clear that she’d respect their decision whatever it was. Despite their long life of public deception, it was hard not to admire them both, especially the man who’d kept his vow and, rather heroically, assisted his sister in her time of difficulty.

Everything finally got the best of Fanny, and she stepped forward and hugged Miss Annie with tears in her eyes.

When she was finished, we all went inside to wait for the others.

48. Denouement

Wednesday, March 21, 1900

Finally, everything was as it should be.

Mr. Frank was back home, my dear doctor was back home, and Sheriff Granger was back in town as well.

Judge Owen Fairfax, sadly enough, had been appropriately eulogized and buried, but I was still burning with unanswered questions, the most predominant being:

Was Ethan Miller my brother?

Or was he my half-brother?

What *exactly* was the relationship between Judge Fairfax and my mother, Rebecca Miller.

Were they lovers?

Was I the "resultant" of an adulterous love affair?

Sheriff Granger initiated:

"Annie's done my job much better than I could have," he announced most graciously to the crowded room of guests that filled up Annie and Frank's living room.

Each and every one of them waiting to hear about the death of dear Miss Dalton.

And *why* it had happened.

Except for me, of course, who already knew.

Annie smiled and deflected.

"This says the man who tracked down the vanished train conductor!"

Everyone laughed.

So, who was everyone?

The guest list was very similar to my original suspect list, with a few additions and omissions.

Mr. Frank
My father
Fanny and the mayor
Their son, Deputy Langley
Sheriff Granger and his son Jimmy
Aaron Anderson and Theresa Morning Dove
Sr. Agnes
Annie
And me

Twelve in all, spread throughout the room, each waiting for Annie to tell them what they needed to hear.

She commenced, as usual, in her soft, careful, and modest voice.

"Fifteen years ago, long before he was the county judge, Owen Fairfax took a compassionate interest in the troubling situation of a young widow, Lizzie's mother. I should say, immediately, that I have no belief that anything illicit ever happened between them."

Meaning adultery.

Annie was clearly letting me know that I should relax, so I did my best.

"Rebecca's husband, Gordon Miller, had died recently in a terrible work accident at Franklin Quarry, and she soon discovered that she was pregnant with her second child, our dear young Lizzie. It was at that point that Rebecca contacted Owen Fairfax, a wills and contract lawyer at the time, to organize her husband's meager but confusing finances. The date was May 15th, 1884, which I know from a notation in the judge's legal records."

She looked over at the sheriff.

"The sheriff and I spent some time this morning in the judge's office."

When the sheriff nodded, Annie looked at Frank, who was sitting beside her. Obviously prepared, Mr. Frank handed her a large black ledger which she opened on her lap, found her place, and read to everyone in the room.

> *May 15, 1884, Thursday, contacted by Mrs. Gordon Miller to legalize the accounts of her deceased husband. A meeting is scheduled next Monday, 2:15.*

Annie closed the book, and Frank removed it from her lap.

"I want to be perfectly clear about this since it verifies the fact that Lizzie's father was Gordon Miller, and that there's no possibility that the judge might have been her father. Mrs. Miller was already pregnant when they met for the first time."

Everyone was relieved and satisfied, most of all me.

I won't attempt to describe the extent of my relief, but I immediately settled back comfortably in my chair, as Annie continued.

"Whatever their subsequent relationship, Owen clearly helped the young widow with Lizzie's birth expenses and even provided the woman with an annual stipend, which, for some reason, he kept secret from his wife, Veronica. Three years later, when Mrs. Miller was murdered by Helen Randolph, Owen redirected the anonymous stipend to Sr. Agnes at the orphanage, where young Lizzie had been taken after the murder of her mother and the abduction of her brother.

"Long after Rebecca's death, Owen Fairfax honored her memory by visiting her grave with flowers on the anniversary of her death."

Annie didn't bother to point out that, to avoid detection, he'd recently fired two bullets over my head nine days ago in the Nutley cemetery.

"As I've recently discovered, ten years ago, Judge Fairfax began paying blackmail in the amount of $200 each month, delivered by courier. His anonymous blackmailer had threatened to expose his supposed 'relationship' with Rebecca Miller, as well as the secret stipend. I must admit that I was quite surprised to discover that the blackmailer was his own wife, Veronica."

Everyone, except for me, of course, and Sheriff Granger, was stunned. There were murmurs of disbelief, as Annie paused a moment before continuing.

"I believe that Veronica had discovered the truth about Owen's secret stipend and immediately assumed the worst, assuming that her husband was probably Lizzie's father. Not wishing to blacken her family in public, yet still wishing to somehow punish her husband, she decided to blackmail him anonymously, and he willingly paid the money."

"Why?" Aaron wondered.

"I believe he did it to prevent a scandal. I believe he did it to protect his two sons, and, ironically, protect his wife. He continued making those payments until the last one on Monday of last week, which was delivered by Jimmy."

Everyone looked at Jimmy.

"I delivered them every month, dropping the envelope off in a makeshift postbox near the Supply Store."

"Which, as we all know," the mayor pointed out, "is owned by Veronica Fairfax."

"Yes," Annie agreed.

As always, Annie was discreet, failing to mention that the money was eventually funneled to the Fairfax sons through the Franklin Trust. There was also no reason to inform the others that the mayor, as director of Franklin Trust, had revealed the transactions involved with Veronica's bank account.

"That probably helps to explain Veronica's 'change' back then," Fanny suggested. "She always said that her miscarriage had darkened her perspective on life, but maybe it was also her suspicions about her husband."

Which might also explain why Mrs. Fairfax had always behaved so oddly towards me, sometimes excessively polite, sometimes excessively distant.

"Where is she now?" Sr. Agnes wondered. "Is she still resting at home?"

Annie looked at the sheriff.

"She was arrested this afternoon," he explained.

Everyone was astonished.

"Why?" asked Fanny, along with several others.

The sheriff looked back at Annie.

"In part, for the murder of Jane Dalton."

Annie explained.

"Veronica had come to believe that Jane had uncovered, within the 'new' documents forwarded from the Newark Library, irrefutable evidence that the judge was Lizzie's father. We all know that Jane could 'keep a secret' better than anyone else in town, but if it was a matter of parentage, as well as a matter of eventual inheritance, then she might have felt obligated to come forward."

"*Was* there any actual evidence in the Newark documents?" the mayor wondered.

"None. Both Lizzie and I read through them all. I have no idea if Veronica tried to talk things over with Jane. But even if she had, she might not have been fully satisfied. In truth, there was only one way to *completely* protect herself and her two sons. So she arranged a daytime meeting with Miss Jane at Centre Bridge, then pushed our dear friend over the edge. When Rusty, Jane's little dog, turned on Veronica, she kicked him in the head and he fell over the edge as well."

The last detail was obviously meant for me, and much appreciated.

"It's hard to believe," Fanny said, "that Veronica could have done such a thing."

The sheriff clarified.

"She's already confessed. She's also confessed to the murder of her husband."

Which, of course, was yet another shocker.

"I took her into custody," the sheriff explained, "right after she returned home from the burial."

Once again, the sheriff and everyone else looked over at Annie.

"I guess she believed that Owen had figured out everything she'd done. That he'd finally realized that his own wife was blackmailing him. That he'd started putting things together."

"But I thought he died of heart failure?" my father asked.

"That's true, Matthew," Annie explained, "but his heart gave out because he was poisoned, as verified by your colleague, Dr. Yorsten from Belleville, who observed the discoloration of the hands and the insides of the mouth."

Actually, it was *Annie* who'd initially recognized the odd discolorations, and who then alerted Dr. Yorsten to pay close attention. Then she'd met with him at the train station on Monday night before the wake. The next morning, she sent Lawrence to Belleville to get the doctor's full report.

She'd already explained all this to me, specifically about the mysterious man at the train station, during our long ride back from Hanover after the arrest of Ethan and Helen Randolph.

"I didn't want you to know," Annie explained on the ride home, "what Veronica had done before the wake."

I understood.

It was hard enough sitting in the house of gloom without being aware of the fact that the man's poor "grieving" wife had actually murdered her husband.

"Veronica used an arsenic compound," Annie explained, "which is sold at the supply store as rat poison."

"Yes," the sheriff confirmed. "And we've found traces inside the house itself."

Annie looked over at Lawrence, who was holding the report.

"Could you read the doctor's conclusion?"

Lawrence read it aloud:

> *In summary, in my professional medical opinion, Owen Fairfax died of heart seizure directly induced by the ingestion of poison arsenic, clearly indicated by the discolorations detailed above. As regarding legal matters, Owen Fairfax's murder was either an unlikely suicide or a homicide, which is best left to both the sheriff's office and the courts. Dr. David Yorsten*

"Which is why it was a closed coffin," Lawrence clarified.

Annie let everything sink in, then she continued.

"There's something else you need to know."

Everyone waited.

"Keith Fairfax has also been arrested."

Once again, Annie looked at the sheriff.

"For assault and forced detainment," he explained, "of Miss Lizzie."

Everyone looked at me.

When Annie nodded, I explained as succinctly as I could.

"During a music break at the Valentine's Day Dance, I was sitting outside Old Military Hall thinking about my brother, when someone assaulted me and covered my head with a burlap bag. Then I was led into the woods, forcibly, where I was threatened to 'Leave well enough alone.'"

"It was Keith and his mother," Annie explained. "She'd convinced him that Lizzie was about to reveal something from the past that would bring shame and scandal on the entire family, and he was foolish and trusting enough to go along."

"Did he have anything to do with his father's death?" the mayor wondered.

"No, he was in New York at the time, as was his brother Bryan, who took no part in any of the unpleasantness with Lizzie."

"It's horrible," Fanny decided.

Everyone agreed.

"Maybe this is a good time," Annie suggested, "to take a break for tea?"

Which was a cue for me and Theresa to serve the other guests fresh tea, lemonade, and Annie's sweet jelly cakes. As we went about our business, there was much chatter in the room. As one might expect. It was hard to believe that "one of our own" had actually been a murderer. Twice. A woman whom everyone knew and respected.

Who was a friend.

Eventually, when things settled down, we moved to Case #2, which, of course, I was dreading, but Annie whispered in my ear:

"It's best to get it over with, my dear."

I knew it was true, and things went as well as they might.

As delicately as possible, Annie described the brutal murder of my mother on the banks of the Passaic River, the subsequent abduction of my brother Ethan, his five years of total confinement in a storage barn, his subsequent years working the farm with his "father" under a fictitious name, and his eventual abandonment in Albany, New York, by Jonas Randolph."

"Why?" Jimmy asked. "Why was he abandoned?"

I could have strangled him.

Even though it was a perfectly logical question.

Annie was deft as always.

"He'd become disillusioned with the boy's behavior."

Well, that's one way to put it! Without delineating the salacious physical extremity of Helen and Ethan's relationship, which was some kind of bizarre and creepy quasi-incest.

"How did he end up in Nutley?" my father wondered.

"He'd heard Mrs. Randolph mention the name of the town," Annie explained, leaving out the part about Helen Randolph having a cousin (the mayor) in town, who was sitting right here in the living room.

Then Annie explained about Ethan's desperate desire to reunite with his mother, his eventual return to Hanover, Helen's subsequent murder of her husband,

and the eventual confrontation and arrest.

"Why did she kill her husband?" Aaron wondered.

"I think she believed that he'd, once again, drive the boy away."

She left it like that.

When all the questions were finally over and answered, the tea and lemonade were joined by sherry and brandy. Everyone was conversing animatedly in small groups, trying to fathom the perfectly unfathomable, yet glad that it was finally over. Despite the odd circumstances, they were still enjoying each other's company. Like Annie, I made the rounds, spending time with everyone, including both Lawrence and Jimmy.

Later, when I was talking with Theresa and Aaron, my father walked over.

He had a glass of something red in his hand.

"I'm very proud of you, Lizzie."

Aaron and Theresa agreed.

As I stood there mute with gratitude, my father smiled.

"Would you like your first glass of sherry?"

He knew I'd been curious about his nightly glass, which he enjoyed so much.

"Of course."

I took the glass, gave him a hug, then retreated to the front door, exiting onto the front porch.

All alone.

The night was cool, yet not intolerable.

I sat down on the swing and thought about my brother Ethan sitting in a jail somewhere. My father had already, most graciously, promised that we could visit Ethan whenever he was settled somewhere.

"What do you think will happen to him?" I'd asked Sherriff Granger earlier.

"Maybe a few months, Lizzie, or maybe more," he speculated. "Attempting to shoot a woman in the back is no small infraction, but he's got a perfectly clean record, and I'm sure that you and Annie will tell what happened in the most favorable light."

But what would happen after that?

I had no idea.

I took a sip of sherry.

It tasted odd and not particularly pleasant. I suppose I'd been attracted by its lovely redness. I placed the glass down on the little table in front of me, as Annie came out the front door.

She was worried about me.

She looked down at the glass of sherry, said nothing, and sat down beside me on the swing. Her presence, as always, was reassuring.

Much, I assume, like a mother's presence.

"You've grown up a lot, Lizzie."

I thought it over.

"I guess I have," I admitted. "Maybe more than I realize."

"You now have a very exciting life in front of you."

"Could it possibly be more exciting than the past ten days?"

Annie smiled.

Then I asked her the question I'd been avoiding asking her for weeks.

"When are you leaving?"

"Next week," she said. "Rehearsals begin in Connecticut on March 29th."

A week and a half away.

"When does the season open?"

"April 16th."

Every year, the Colonel initiated his Wild West tour with a huge parade in New York City, which was followed by several weeks of shows in Brooklyn before the cross-county tour got under way, usually lasting until September.

When I'd be off at Bryn Mawr.

I looked at Annie directly.

"Take me with you."

She was stunned, and Mrs. Annie Butler was a person who was seldom stunned.

"Just for a few weeks," I pleaded, "I'd like to see a bit of the world before I go off to college in the fall."

"Are you sure?"

"Yes, I could help on the road. Or help Theresa."

"It's not as glamourous as it might seem, Lizzie. Mostly we sleep in tents and railroad cars."

"I grew up in an orphanage, Miss Annie. It sounds rather wonderful."

"All right," she decided. "I'll talk to your father."

"Whose goal in life is to spoil me to death!"

She laughed.

"What about Mr. Frank?" I wondered.

"Well, we both know that he's spoiler number two!"

I gave her a hug.

"Let's see what happens," she whispered.

Annie stood up, bent over, and kissed me on the forehead. Then she opened the front door and reentered her home.

Everything seemed right again.

Tomorrow will be even better.

Tomorrow, Annie and I will go riding again!

William Baer is the award-winning author of more than thirty books including the Jack Colt mystery series *New Jersey Noir*, the Deirdre Flanagan mystery series, *Companion*, *Advocatus Diaboli*, *Times Square and Other Stories*, *Classic American Films*, and *One-and-Twenty Tales*. A graduate of Rutgers, NYU, South Carolina, the Johns Hopkins Writing Seminars, and USC Cinema, he's been the recipient of a Guggenheim Fellowship, a Fulbright (Portugal), an NEA fellowship in fiction, and the Jack Nicholson Screenwriting Award. He lives happily in a log cabin in the lake region of north New Jersey.

Made in the USA
Middletown, DE
15 July 2024

57311986R00168